The Two Presidents

Joseph Boro

Published by Boro Publishing, LLC, 2024.

THE TWO PRESIDENTS

First edition. February 29, 2024.

Copyright © 2024 Joseph Boro.

ISBN: 979-8989859207

Written by Joseph Boro.

Table of Contents

For the dreamers, and those who wonder

Chapter 1

Atoms and Rockets

LOS ALAMOS, NEW MEXICO, USA

Ninety seconds ticked away in tense anticipation as Dr. Robert Oppenheimer observed from a distance, his eyes fixed on the completion of a weapon destined to reshape the course of history—the atom bomb. As technicians meticulously added the finishing touches, the weight of its potential consequences hung in the air. Adjusting his goggles, Oppenheimer braced himself, acutely aware that the successful activation of this weapon could alter the very fabric of the world.

The countdown echoed in his ears, each second a palpable reminder of the monumental task at hand. Sixty seconds remained, and Oppenheimer, the brilliant scientist who had invested his essence into the creation of this device, could almost feel the collective breath of humanity held in suspense. Blood, sweat, and tears had been poured into the atomic crucible, and now the precipice of either global destruction or a new era of warfare loomed before him.

Thirty seconds. The point of no return. The dawn of the atomic age awaited, and Oppenheimer steeled himself for the irreversible transformation about to unfold. As the countdown reached its zenith, the scientist, his goggles tightly secured, found a moment to hold his breath—a deep inhalation before the precipitous plunge into the unknown.

Ten seconds. The culmination of years of research and scientific endeavor. Almost there, almost there. The final five seconds marked the descent into an unimaginable future as the world teetered on the brink of an unprecedented technological leap.

The detonation unfolded in a blinding flash of light, an enormous fireball heralding the birth of destructive power beyond comprehension. Moments passed before the shockwave reverberated through the atmosphere, a terrible force that shook Oppenheimer to his core. In the aftermath, the weight of realization dawned upon him—what had he unleashed upon the world? Was he, in the words of ancient scripture, become death, the destroyer of worlds?

As Oppenheimer grappled with the gravity of his creation, jubilation erupted among the other attendees. Cheers filled the air, a celebration of scientific achievement and the creation of the atom bomb. Yet, their joy was not a proclamation of victory in a world at war; instead, it was the affirmation of a new kind of power, a deterrent capable of reshaping geopolitical landscapes.

Unbeknownst to the world, this pivotal test had not occurred on July 16th, 1945, as in our history, but on December 6th, 1941. The fabric of time had been rewoven, altering the course of events. How had this transpired? The answer lay in the winds of change, stirred by a mysterious advisor who had emerged to counsel the president. This enigmatic figure, shrouded in secrecy, played a pivotal role in steering the hands of fate, ushering in an alternate reality where the atom bomb's genesis intersected with a fateful date in December 1941. The world stood on the precipice of an unfamiliar era, shaped by the choices of those who dared to defy the constraints of destiny.

SEATED BEHIND HIS DESK, President Franklin D. Roosevelt delved into the latest newspaper, absorbing the grim updates on the beleaguered state of Britain in the throes of war-torn Europe. Despite the challenging circumstances, the resilience of the British was evident, buoyed in part by the substantial aid dispatched from the United States. Roosevelt found solace in the knowledge that he served as a persistent thorn in Adolf Hitler's side, a testament to the power of American support. He also was heartened by the latest report that the Jewish settlement he sponsored in Alaska was going well.

As the President contemplated the precarious state of affairs, the black phone on his desk jolted him from his musings, its insistent ringing demanding attention. With measured movements, Roosevelt reached for the receiver.

"Hello?" he answered, his voice a blend of authority and curiosity. "Yes. I understand. That is excellent news. Please prepare a report for when manufacturing of more can take place."

The president hung up, a quiet satisfaction marking his demeanor. The atom bomb test had proven successful, and the United States now stood as the world's sole nuclear power, a formidable force even as it maintained a stance of neutrality in the ongoing war—a precarious equilibrium, at least for the time being.

Reaching for the phone once more, Roosevelt dialed his secretary. "Missy, please contact Mr. Mason; I require his presence." The call concluded, and the president leaned back in his chair, reflecting on the peculiar journey that had led him into the orbit of this mysterious figure.

Thoughts ebbed and flowed through Roosevelt's mind as he considered the enigma that was Frederik Mason. A man of veiled influence and cryptic connections, Mr. Mason had proven instrumental in steering the course of events that now found the United States at the forefront of nuclear prowess. The president marveled at the intricacies of fate that had intertwined their paths, wondering how such an unusual alliance had come to fruition.

As the wheels of communication turned, Roosevelt awaited the arrival of Mr. Mason, a man whose presence signified both opportunity and uncertainty. The war-torn world hung in the balance, and the president, now privy to the success of the atom bomb test, understood that the dynamics of global power were about to undergo a seismic shift—one in which he and Frederick played pivotal roles.

8 YEARS EARLIER, GERMANY, 1934

Within the convivial ambiance of a German bar, Wernher Von Braun reveled in the jubilation of completing his physics doctorate.

As he savored the moment, a mysterious figure caught his attention—a man conspicuously out of place, sporting a fedora and trench coat. Sensing intrigue, Von Braun turned his gaze towards the enigmatic visitor.

"Guten Tag, Herr Von Braun," the mysterious man greeted in German.

"Guten Tag. Do I know you?" Von Braun responded in kind.

A sly smile played on the man's lips. "No, no, I suppose you wouldn't. My name is Herr Mr. Mason, and I represent the Roosevelt administration."

"Roosevelt? An American? Why are you here?" questioned Von Braun, raising an eyebrow, his curiosity piqued.

"I've come to offer you a job," Mr. Mason said smoothly, gesturing for Von Braun to take a seat at a nearby table.

"And why me exactly? Don't you have your own rocket scientist? Dr. Goddard is well known, even here in Germany," Von Braun remarked.

Mr. Mason shrugged with an air of nonchalance. "Ehhh, Dr. Goddard has... personal issues. So, I've come to recruit the next best—you."

"Me?" Von Braun exclaimed in surprise. "Why, I'm no one. I literally just obtained my PhD. I'm sure there are more experienced engineers you can turn to."

Mr. Mason chuckled. "Your reputation precedes you. President Roosevelt requested you specifically, along with your entire team. Your brother, your colleagues, all of them."

"Really?" Von Braun uttered again, taken aback. "And why would I, I presume, travel all the way to America when I can pursue my work here in Germany?"

Leaning forward to ensure privacy, Mr. Mason beckoned Von Braun to do the same. "President Roosevelt plans to announce a new work program with an audacious goal in mind—to land a man on the moon."

Von Braun's eyes widened. "The moon? The Americans want to go to the moon?"

"Oh yes."

"And how did the president come to this decision?" inquired Von Braun, intrigued.

Mr. Mason smiled enigmatically. "Let's say, I can be persuasive."

Von Braun stared at Mr. Mason, realizing the extraordinary influence wielded by this mysterious man.

"I, uh... I need to talk to my team first," Von Braun finally asserted.

Mr. Mason leaned back. "Of course, just give me a call when you make a decision." He handed Von Braun a small card. "The phone number for the hotel I'm staying at is on the back."

With that, Mr. Mason gracefully exited, leaving Wernher Von Braun in a state of speechless contemplation. "The moon," he murmured to himself, recognizing the rarity of such a profound opportunity. It would take quite a bit of convincing, but he thinks he could get it done.

—————————

8 YEARS LATER, WASHINGTON D.C

"Are you certain that we can still trust Dr. Von Braun?" President Roosevelt's question hung in the air of the Senate chamber as he sat in his wheelchair, eyes fixed on the balding man in a suit and tie standing beside him. "John is growing increasingly concerned about his loyalties, advocating for closer scrutiny."

Frederick Mason, the man Roosevelt addressed, acknowledged the concern with a nod. "Understandable, given Germany's attempts to subjugate Europe."

Roosevelt's brow furrowed in contemplation. "You may know the events that transpired, but your interventions have already altered the course of things, and I'm uncertain if it's for the better."

"Trust me, it is."

"You don't know that!"

"I have a pretty good idea."

The president continued to frown. "Then you best ensure it."

Mason smiled confidently. "Don't worry; you'll get your war soon. You just have to wait for tomorrow."

Roosevelt sighed heavily, an air of foreboding in the room. "God help us all." He wheeled over to a liquor cabinet, pouring himself some gin.

"If they heed the warnings, things will go more smoothly this time," Mason reassured.

"We can only hope," Roosevelt said, downing the drink without bothering to prepare it properly. "Why don't you head back to the enclave? It's going to be a long day tomorrow."

"Of course, Mr. President," Mason replied, turning to leave. "Have a good evening."

"Same to you, Mr. President." As the door closed behind Mason, Roosevelt sat alone in contemplation, the weight of impending events pressing down on him. The room seemed filled with the gravity of decisions yet to unfold, and the president grappled with the uncertainty that accompanied this altered course of history. In the solitude of his office, Roosevelt pondered the intricate dance of fate and the consequences of tampering with the natural order of time.

Chapter 2

Infamy

DECEMBER 7th, 1941

8 AM

Admiral Nagumo, at the helm of the first air fleet, stared intently at the horizon. The planes should have reached Honolulu by now, engaged in the ruthless destruction of the American Pacific fleet. Anticipation knotted in his stomach as he awaited news of the attack's success or failure, the fate of the Japanese Empire was hanging in the balance.

In a moment that seemed to stretch into eternity, he drew a deep breath. Suddenly, the world around him convulsed. The once-steady deck beneath his feet betrayed him, and Admiral Nagumo found himself sprawled on the floor, ears ringing from an unseen force. Alarms blared, the disconcerting symphony of chaos filling the air as the ship groaned and creaked around him.

"What happened?" he pondered, his thoughts drowned by the cacophony of the unfolding disaster. "Was that an explosion?" A glance to his uniform revealed ominous stains of blood, a surreal tableau of violence etched onto the fabric.

Explosions echoed outside, mingling with the urgent shouts of sailors in Japanese. Turning to the space he had occupied moments earlier, Admiral Nagumo's eyes widened in disbelief at the sight of a massive hole, a testament to the destructive force that had just pierced through their vessel.

Summoning every ounce of strength, he heaved himself back onto unsteady legs. Peering through the wreckage, his eyes widened further as he beheld a squadron of planes attacking them. A closer inspection revealed U.S. markings on their fuselages.

Admiral Nagumo's shock transformed into a realization that chilled him to the core. "They knew. The Americans knew!" he muttered, a sense of profound dread settling in. "They were prepared and were waiting to be attacked first. By God, what have we done?"

Bleeding profusely, the admiral struggled to maintain his composure. As he stood over the gaping hole in the ship, he felt the warmth of his own blood seeping through his uniform. In a moment of profound weakness, the weight of his actions and the unforeseen consequences bore down on him.

With that last haunting thought, Admiral Nagumo succumbed to unconsciousness, his body giving way as he fell forward onto the unforgiving deck below. The once-confident commander of a devastating attack now lay defeated, the grim reality of war exacting its toll on both sides of the conflict.

ADMIRAL HUSBAND KIMMEL found himself reluctantly standing on the bridge of the USS Lexington. The urgency of the situation weighed heavily on him, as his command at Pearl Harbor faced a relentless onslaught. The presidential order compelled his presence here, even in the midst of active attack, and he braced himself for the grim tidings that awaited.

"Admiral Kimmel," a young ensign saluted as he approached. "The latest report from Pearl, sir," he said, extending a piece of paper to the admiral.

Taking the report, Kimmel's eyes quickly scanned the disheartening details. "Most of the Japanese attack wave destroyed, several hundred U.S. planes lost, and a crashing Zero causing damage to our fuel depots. Shit, the Arizona is a total loss with a massive loss of life."

A wave of despair washed over the admiral, and he staggered, placing a hand to his temple. The magnitude of the disaster was apparent. However, amid the devastation, there was a glimmer of solace – a significant portion of the Japanese air fleet had been crippled. Kimmel knew he needed to return to Pearl Harbor promptly to assess the full extent of the damage.

"Captain, how soon before we can make way for Pearl?" Kimmel inquired, the urgency evident in his voice.

"As soon as our last planes return," the Captain responded. "So far, the returning pilots have reported a complete success in their operation."

"By how much?" Kimmel asked, a courtesy disguising his inner turmoil.

"All six aircraft carriers have been sunk, along with all their cruisers, destroyers, and tankers," the Captain reported. "They did mention, however, that they could not locate the light cruiser that intelligence said would be there."

Kimmel took a deep breath, absorbing the information. "Hopefully this victory will satisfy their need for revenge. They did succeed in sinking the Arizona at her berth."

The captain's eyes widened in realization. "Oh, fuck."

"I know. I'm the one who has to report this to the president," Kimmel admitted grimly.

Together, the two naval officers watched as the last planes returned from their daring bombing run on the Japanese fleet. The air hung heavy with the aftermath of battle, a silent testament to the sacrifices made and the tumultuous course of history that unfolded that fateful day.

PRESIDENT FRANKLIN Roosevelt's countenance darkened as he listened intently on the phone, absorbing the weight of the information conveyed.

"Yes, yes... I understand. Thank you for this information," he uttered into the receiver before gently placing it back on its cradle. A sigh escaped him as he pressed a hand to his temple, the gravity of the news settling heavily on his shoulders.

"Good news or bad news?" Frederick Mason inquired, the only other presence in the room.

"A bit of both," Roosevelt responded with a heavy sigh. "Most of the attacking Japanese fleet has been destroyed, but we have sustained heavy losses."

"What kind of losses?" Mr. Mason questioned, raising an eyebrow.

"The USS Arizona was completely destroyed, most of her crew lost," Roosevelt said solemnly. "Along with several hundred planes burning on the tarmac, and the fuel depots."

"Damn it," Mr. Mason cursed, slamming his fist on the desk.

"At least 1,400 killed or injured, possibly many more." In that moment, Roosevelt seemed to age twenty years, the toll of the tragic losses etched into his expression.

"Any other ships lost?" Mason inquired.

"No, just the Arizona."

"Well, it could have been worse."

"Really?" Roosevelt asked, his disbelief evident.

"Oh yes, far worse, for the fleet and in lives lost. I think we got off lucky, and now you have a justifiable cause for war to present to Congress."

"Yes, but at what cost," Roosevelt said gravely. "The country was attacked, young men are dead or permanently injured."

"Things are far worse in Europe. The evil that is going on there..." Mr. Mason shuddered at the thought.

"When will Dr. Von Braun's aircraft be ready?" Roosevelt redirected the conversation, a necessary pivot in the face of adversity.

"April or May."

"Then we should get on it. That is all," Roosevelt declared.

Mr. Mason simply nodded before turning and leaving the room. The weight of the decisions made and those yet to be faced hung in the air, and Roosevelt, grappling with the aftermath of the attack on Pearl Harbor, knew that the path ahead was fraught with challenges and sacrifices.

THE FOLLOWING DAY, Franklin Delano Roosevelt, the President of the United States, addressed the nation and a somber Congress in a historic speech that would resonate through the annals of history. It was a day etched in collective memory, December 7th, 1941, a day of infamy that would galvanize the American people and shape the course of world events.

In the echoing chambers of the Capitol, Roosevelt's voice carried the weight of determination and resolve. He painted a vivid picture of the audacious attack that had transpired, emphasizing the unjust violation of American sovereignty. The President acknowledged the valor of U.S. forces, who had successfully crippled most of the Japanese fleet responsible for the assault. However, he made it unequivocally clear that this was not the end; it was a call to finish what had been started.

With a steely resolve in his eyes, Roosevelt stood before Congress and the nation, seeking not just retribution but a commitment to justice. He called upon the representatives to unite and defend the principles for which the United States stood. In the face of this unprovoked aggression, he did not mince words—asking for a declaration of war against Japan.

Within the hallowed halls of Congress, a few hours later, the response was swift. The representatives, reflecting the sentiment of an outraged nation, granted Roosevelt's request. The United States, once committed to neutrality, had now been thrust into the crucible of war.

As the declaration of war resonated through the corridors of power, a solemn gravity descended upon the nation. The radio waves carried the weight of the President's words into homes across the country, as families gathered around to absorb the magnitude of the moment. Flags flew at half-mast, and a palpable sense of determination swept through the air.

The United States, awakened from its peace, was now propelled into the maelstrom of global conflict. The attack on Pearl Harbor had not only left a scar on the Pacific Fleet but had ignited a fire in the hearts of the American people. Germany, Italy and Japan had no idea what was in store for them.

United States Declares War on Japan After Failed Pearl Harbor Attack, Japanese Fleet Wiped Out

By Anthony Bridger
December 8, 1941

In an unprecedented move that has shocked the world, President Franklin D. Roosevelt addressed the nation today, announcing that the United States is officially entering the World War following the devastating surprise attack on Pearl Harbor. The declaration of war comes on the heels of a meticulously coordinated assault by the Imperial Japanese Navy that targeted the heart of the U.S. Pacific Fleet.

Early on the morning of December 7, 1941, Japanese forces launched a surprise aerial assault on the U.S. naval base at Pearl Harbor, Hawaii. The meticulously planned attack unfolded with precision, catching the American forces off guard. The attackers focused primarily on crippling the Pacific Fleet, targeting battleships, cruisers, and destroyers docked in the harbor.

The results of the assault were catastrophic for the United States. The surprise attack left the U.S. Pacific Fleet in shambles, with several battleships, cruisers, and destroyers either sunk or heavily damaged. The devastation extended beyond the military infrastructure, reaching civilian areas, and the loss of life was substantial. The attack on Pearl Harbor claimed the lives of over 2,400 Americans and wounded more than 1,000 others.

President Roosevelt, addressing a joint session of Congress on December 8, 1941, delivered a stirring speech that would be etched into the annals of history. In his address, Roosevelt condemned the "day that will live in infamy" and declared that the United States was officially entering the global conflict. The President stated, "No matter how long it may take us to overcome this premeditated invasion, the American people in their righteous might will win through to absolute victory."

The announcement was met with a groundswell of support from the American public, with citizens rallying behind the decision to enter the war. In response to the unprovoked aggression, Congress swiftly and overwhelmingly passed a formal declaration of war against the Empire of Japan.

Simultaneously, reports from the Pacific theater are already revealing a turning tide in the conflict. While the Japanese attack on Pearl Harbor was intended to cripple the U.S. Pacific Fleet and buy time for Japan's territorial expansion, the unforeseen resilience of American forces and the imminent entry of the United States into the war present a formidable challenge for the Axis powers.

In a dramatic turn of events, reports indicate that the Japanese fleet, responsible for the assault on Pearl Harbor, has suffered significant losses. U.S. forces, scrambling to respond, reportedly engaged and inflicted heavy damage on the Japanese naval fleet, effectively wiping it out in a retaliatory strike. This unexpected counteraction underscores the resilience and determination of the United States to confront and overcome the aggression inflicted upon them.

As the world braces for the consequences of the United States' entry into the World War, one thing remains certain – the events of December 7, 1941, and the subsequent declaration of war have reshaped the course of history, setting the stage for a global conflict that will test the strength and resolve of nations across the globe.

WINSTON CHURCHILL, the indomitable Prime Minister of the United Kingdom, found himself grappling with a perplexing reality. The intelligence reports had all pointed in the same direction—Adolf Hitler declaring war on the United States within days. Yet, despite the ominous anticipation, there was an unexpected delay, and the United States remained officially at peace with Germany.

While Churchill recognized that the long-term inevitability of war loomed, the short-term implications were far more troublesome, if not disastrous. The delay threatened to hinder the inflow of crucial U.S. aid, a lifeline desperately needed as Britain braced for a protracted struggle against the Axis powers.

THE TWO PRESIDENTS

Sitting in his office, Churchill mulled over the geopolitical chessboard that now spanned the globe. U.S. aid was now reserved for the war effort against Japan on the opposite side of the world. Although the nations remained allies in the Pacific theater, Churchill foresaw a challenging situation where resources would be diverted, leaving the European front in a precarious position.

Pouring himself a generous glass of brandy, Churchill sought solace in the amber liquid, contemplating the turbulent times ahead. The diplomatic dance between the United States and Germany had placed Britain in a strategic conundrum. While they could still draw support for the fight against Japan and extract resources for the European theater, the lack of an official declaration of war posed complications.

Churchill, pragmatic and forward-thinking, acknowledged the importance of making the alliance with the United States official. Such a move would be a godsend in securing the resources and support needed for the broader war effort. With a wry smile, he raised his glass in a toast to the hope that the geopolitical knots tying Britain's fate would soon unravel.

As the brandy warmed his insides, Churchill reflected on the gravity of the situation. The fate of Europe hung in the balance, and the role of the United States was paramount. Much more than he had let on in his conversations with Franklin, Churchill understood the pivotal role America played. In the quiet solitude of his office, he muttered a quiet prayer, "God help us all."

ADOLF HITLER SIMMERED with rage, his fury barely contained as he resisted the impulse to hurl his advisor out the window and onto the bustling street below. Despite his initial inclination to dismiss the counsel, the advisor had made a salient point—one that demanded Hitler's begrudging acknowledgment.

Their Japanese allies had indeed struck a monumental blow against the United States, yet the cost was steep. A substantial portion of the Japanese fleet lay crippled in the aftermath. Their appearance of strength was a mere façade; beneath it, vulnerability festered. The advisor argued that the United States, though appearing formidable, was weakened, their posture a strategic deception.

Moreover, the advisor presented a compelling perspective on seizing a new opportunity that would wound Britain. With the Americans entangled in the Pacific theater against Japan, their attention and resources would be diverted. The flow of aid to Britain, a lifeline in their struggle against the Allied forces, would wither. Patience, the advisor insisted, was the key—to let the Americans exhaust themselves in a war of attrition against Japan.

However, Hitler's simmering anger found a new focal point. American ships were now retaliating against German U-boats. The provocations could not be ignored. The desire for immediate retaliation pulsed through Hitler's veins, but a more calculated side of him recognized the strategic importance of biding their time.

For now, Germany would assume a watching stance. The spring would bring a decisive moment, a juncture where they would evaluate the geopolitical landscape and make a critical decision—whether to plunge into war against the United States or remain in the shadows, leveraging the distraction created by the conflict in the Pacific.

As Hitler reluctantly acquiesced to the advisor's counsel, the war machine of Nazi Germany paused momentarily. The wheels of decision turned slowly, and the fate of nations hung in the balance.

The world would soon witness whether Hitler's restraint would prove to be a tactical masterstroke or a hesitant misstep on the precipice of global conflict.

Chapter 3

Retaliation

ROSWELL, NEW MEXICO, March 1942

Dr. Wernher Von Braun swiped the beads of sweat from his brow under the relentless desert sun, immersed in his work within the expansive hangar. Seven years in the United States had molded him into a patriot of sorts, a sentiment that resonated within the vast expanse of his adopted homeland. Despite the admiration he harbored for his new country, he couldn't shake the occasional skeptical glance from detractors. He understood their suspicions; had he stayed in Germany, he might be toiling under the oppressive regime of the S.S instead of the U.S. Army.

Safety and opportunity beckoned to him in the United States, where he pursued his dream project with fervor, at least during peacetime. As Von Braun immersed himself in the complexities of his work, he was abruptly pulled from his thoughts by the arrival of two unexpected visitors – a uniformed man and a familiar face, a balding man in a suit and tie. The latter he recognized immediately.

"Good afternoon, Dr. Von Braun," the uniformed man greeted. "Allow me to introduce you to Mr. Frederick Mason, advisor to the president."

"This isn't our first meeting," Von Braun replied in English, though his German accent lingered. He extended a hand to Mason. "Mr. Mason is the one who recruited me in the first place."

"Oh, really?" the uniformed man expressed surprise. "You certainly get around, Mr. Mason."

"Yes indeed," Mason replied with a grin.

"I assume this isn't a personal visit?" Von Braun inquired.

"No," Mason responded, shaking his head. "I'm here on behalf of President Roosevelt. He wants an update on when your craft will be ready."

"Ah, about two weeks, give or take depending on the weather," Von Braun replied, gesturing toward the aircraft beside him.

"What is that thing, anyway?" the uniformed soldier queried with curiosity.

"Ah, I'm afraid that is classified," Mason interjected.

"As is much about you, Mr. Mason," Von Braun added.

"Indeed," Mason acknowledged.

Sighing in defeat at not getting a satisfactory answer, the soldier gestured, "Come on, I'll escort you out of here."

"It's been a pleasure to meet you again, Mr. Mason. Perhaps we'll do so one more time under better circumstances," Von Braun suggested.

"Perhaps at the moon launch," Mason proposed.

"Oh yes," Von Braun said dreamily. "That is the whole point of me coming to America, is it not? Perhaps it can still go on while the war rages."

Mason shrugged. "Perhaps. I'll suggest it to President Roosevelt as a possible morale booster since much of it is already built. Good luck, Dr. Von Braun."

"As to you, Mr. Mason." With that, Von Braun returned to his work, focusing on constructing a rocket-powered bomber aircraft, his mind already reaching toward the future. In two weeks, Japan would know what had hit her.

COLONEL JAMES DOOLITTLE stood resolute on the deck of the USS Hornet, a commanding figure overseeing the aircraft that would soon be under his control. The enormity of the mission weighed heavily on his mind, and he couldn't help but express his discontent aloud.

"I don't know what they were thinking," he lamented, his voice carrying across the deck.

His bombardier, aware of the gravity of the situation, responded, "I believe they wanted to drop a 9000-pound payload on Japan, on a plane designed to carry only 2000 pounds."

Doolittle, clearly irritated, retorted, "That was a rhetorical question."

"Sorry," the bomber said sheepishly, recognizing the need to tread lightly.

"No, don't apologize, no need," Doolittle said, a tinge of dejection in his tone. "I kinda wish we went for the original plan of an entire squadron run with... I guess I should call them 'normal' bombs? It seemed so much simpler."

"I can see the reasoning behind this decision," the bomber offered. "With this plan, it's just two crews risking their lives instead of sixteen. Plus, it kicks Japan while it's down and serves as a warning to the Germans."

"We're not even at war with the Germans," Doolittle pointed out.

"Yeah, but it's a lot closer than it's not," the bomber replied.

"True," Doolittle conceded with a shrug. He then decides to change the subject. "Do me a favor and ask the captain when we can launch."

"Yes, sir," the bombardier responded, snapping off a salute before hurrying off towards the bridge.

Taking a moment to collect himself, Doolittle drew in a deep breath and sighed. "The world was about to change, whether they wanted it to or not. Let's do this thing."

CONFIDENTIAL MILITARY REPORT

To: President Franklin D. Roosevelt

From: Colonel James Doolittle

Subject: Strategic Aerial Operations – Operation Retribution Follow-Up and Atomic Bombing of Hiroshima and Tokyo

Date: April 18, 1942

Mr. President,

I hope this report finds you in good health and high spirits. I write to provide a comprehensive account of recent strategic aerial operations undertaken by the United States Army Air Forces under my command.

1. Operation Retribution Follow-Up:

Following the successful execution of the Operation Retribution, I am pleased to report that our aircrews displayed exceptional courage and determination. The surprise nature of the raid achieved its intended objectives, striking a significant blow against the morale and strategic capabilities of the Japanese Empire. Our pilots demonstrated remarkable skill and resilience, successfully delivering a substantial payload on Japanese targets. Intelligence gathered indicates a tangible impact on the enemy's war effort.

2. Atomic Bombing of Hiroshima and Tokyo:

Subsequently, our military initiated a groundbreaking operation employing a new and potent weapon – the atomic bomb. On April 18, 1942, the city of Hiroshima was subjected to the destructive force of this unprecedented device. The devastation caused by the atomic bomb is beyond our initial estimations, with reports confirming severe damage to infrastructure, military installations, and, unfortunately, civilian populations.

Furthermore, a second atomic bomb was deployed over Tokyo. The target selection aimed at dismantling key elements of the Japanese war machine. The impact was catastrophic, with widespread destruction observed in the target areas.

3. Intelligence and Analysis:

Preliminary intelligence assessments suggest that the use of atomic weaponry has forced the Japanese Imperial High Command into a position of reconsideration regarding their continued prosecution of the war. The strategic implications of these attacks cannot be overstated, as the unprecedented power of atomic weapons has ushered in a new era of warfare.

4. Casualties and Humanitarian Considerations:

The unfortunate reality of such devastating operations is the loss of life, both military and civilian. Detailed casualty reports are forthcoming, but it is clear that the toll has been significant. In the pursuit of military objectives, we must acknowledge the human cost and consider the long-term implications on the global stage.

5. Recommendations:

The successful deployment of atomic weapons prompts us to carefully evaluate the potential for their continued use. I recommend a comprehensive strategic review and discussions on the ethical and political ramifications of this new class of weaponry.

Mr. President, I assure you that every effort has been made to fulfill our duties with unwavering commitment to the principles of democracy and the defense of our great nation. I stand ready to provide further information and analysis as required.

Respectfully,

Colonel James Doolittle

United States Army Air Forces

EMPEROR HIROHITO STOOD amidst the desolation that once was Tokyo, his gaze transfixed on the ruins that mirrored the inevitable devastation that had befallen Hiroshima. The weight of his decisions bore down heavily upon him, and the heavenly solemnity in his countenance teetered on the brink of open despair. What had his advisors persuaded him to unleash upon his own nation?

Never before in Japan's storied history had its sacred soil been violated by an enemy's aggression. Yet, here were the Americans, executing a bold strike mere months after the nation had entered into a catastrophic war. The aftermath of Pearl Harbor, coupled with the unfathomable destruction wrought by these twin bombings—however one might choose to characterize them—left the Imperial Japanese Navy in tatters. The once-mighty army now languished in chaos, its ranks openly clamoring for retribution.

The emperor, despite understanding the fervor within his ranks, harbored doubts about the feasibility of their vengeance. The audacity of the American assault had shattered any illusion of invincibility, leaving Hirohito to grapple with the stark reality that victory seemed an elusive dream. The world, it seemed, had declared war against his empire, and the Americans, relentless and determined, were demanding unconditional surrender.

With a heavy heart, Emperor Hirohito turned away from the somber scene before him, his steps carrying him back toward the imperial palace. Along the way, he paused briefly to address a messenger, a bearer of a message that symbolized the humbling acknowledgment of Japan's dire straits.

"Tell the general staff to initiate negotiations for surrender," the emperor commanded, his voice betraying the gravity of the moment.

Before the messenger could utter another word, Hirohito, the sovereign ruler of Japan, continued his solitary journey, burdened by the weight of a nation in turmoil. The path ahead was fraught with uncertainty, and the echoes of defeat reverberated in every step.

Japan Surrenders After Doolittle Raider Drops Nuclear Bomb on Hiroshima and Tokyo

By Anthony Bridger
April 21, 1942

In a stunning turn of events that has sent shockwaves across the globe, Japan officially surrendered to Allied forces following the deployment of a nuclear bomb on the cities of Hiroshima and Tokyo. The historic surrender, announced by Emperor Hirohito himself, marks a decisive moment in the war.

The unexpected development traces its roots back to April 1942 when Colonel James Doolittle, undertook a perilous mission to deliver a nuclear bomb over Japanese cities.

Doolittle's dual bomber's successfully infiltrated Japanese airspace, overcoming formidable defenses, and dropped the nuclear bomb on Hiroshima, followed by a second bomb on the capital city of Tokyo. The devastating impact of the atomic bombs surpassed anything previously witnessed in the history of warfare, leaving both cities in ruins and instigating widespread panic.

The destructive power of the nuclear weapons proved to be a game-changer, forcing Japan to reevaluate its stance in the face of an imminent and unprecedented threat. The Allied forces, particularly the United States, had unveiled a weapon capable of unparalleled devastation, pushing Japan to the brink of surrender.

In a historic broadcast on April 20, 1942, Emperor Hirohito addressed the Japanese people, announcing the decision to surrender unconditionally. The emperor, who had been a symbol of unwavering determination, now conveyed a somber acknowledgment of Japan's precarious position. "The destructive force unleashed upon us is beyond our capacity to endure. In the interest of our people and the world, we must cease hostilities," declared Hirohito in a speech that reverberated across the war-torn nation.

The surrender of Japan marks the end of the war in the pacific, bringing relief to countless Allied soldiers and civilians who have endured the hardships of the conflict. The Doolittle Raider's daring mission, culminating in the deployment of nuclear weapons, has undeniably shifted the dynamics of the war, prompting a reevaluation of strategies and hastening the pursuit of peace.

As the world grapples with the implications of this unprecedented turn of events, the surrender of Japan stands as a testament to the extraordinary advancements in warfare and the enduring impact of technological innovation on the course of history. The postwar era now beckons, presenting a new set of challenges and opportunities for nations to rebuild and forge a path towards a more peaceful future.

Chapter 4

Peace for Now

PRESIDENT FRANKLIN Roosevelt sat in the Oval Office, a mixture of concern and a lack of surprise etched across his features. The news had reached him – Japan was ready to surrender. However, the lack of movement on the part of Germany and Italy weighed heavily on his mind. Leaning back in his chair, he ran his fingers over his forehead and took a deep, contemplative breath.

After a few moments of silent reflection, he reached for the phone and summoned his secretary. "Missy, please let Mr. Mason know I require his presence," he instructed before hanging up.

Once again, Roosevelt found himself pressing his hands to his temples. The geopolitical landscape was rapidly shifting, and the implications of the situation were unsettling, particularly for Europe. As the leader of a nation that had just secured victory in a few months with minimal casualties, a stark contrast to the expected lengthy war with significant casualties, he grappled with the magnitude of the unfolding events.

In a quiet moment of introspection, Roosevelt offered a silent prayer for the people of Europe. The veil of war still hung over them, a persistent shadow under which they persevered. He empathized with their suffering, well aware of the atrocities committed by the Germans. Mr. Mason, his trusted source, had relayed these distressing accounts, and Roosevelt, though confident in the veracity of the facts, was beginning to doubt the effectiveness of his plans for achieving his goals for the world.

His plans were progressing, but the factual reality of the ongoing struggle in Europe demanded his attention and empathy. In that moment, as the world teetered on the precipice of change, Roosevelt hoped for a swift end to the suffering and an era of lasting peace for the entire world, and not just the U.S.

THE FÜHRER'S OFFICE was fraught with tension as Adolf Hitler raged, his anger palpable to the advisors who stood in silence, unwilling to provoke his wrath. His usual demeanor of calculated authority had given way to genuine fury, an unsettling departure from the norm. The three advisors exchanged uneasy glances, acutely aware that challenging or interrupting him could have severe consequences.

"They are cowards!" Hitler bellowed in German, his voice echoing through the room. "They are not worthy of calling us their ally. Two bombings from some mongrels, and they just give up?!" The dictator, uncharacteristically agitated, spat on the ground in a display of disdain.

In the midst of this tempest, one of the advisors summoned the courage to speak. "Mein Führer," he began cautiously, prompting skeptical glances from his colleagues, "Tokyo has advised that... the bombings were atomic in nature. That is why they are surrendering."

Hitler's furious gaze shifted to the advisor who dared to speak, and he responded with an unsettling coldness. "They lie. It is impossible for an unclean nation like America to develop such a weapon so quickly. Germans will be the ones to develop it first."

The advisor who had spoken retreated into a meek silence. None dared to challenge Hitler's declaration, and the room remained thick with tension as the Führer brooded on his plans.

"We... I... will be declaring war on the Americans soon," Hitler declared with a chilling resolve. "They deserve it. But I am willing to give them a good reason. Begin to brainstorm ways we can strike on their homeland."

With that ominous pronouncement, Adolf Hitler abruptly turned and left the room, leaving his three advisors alone with standing orders. The weight of the task ahead settled on them, and they grappled with the uncertainty of how to fulfill their leader's demands. The challenge was clear – they could not afford to fail in this mission.

"FRED," FRANKLIN ROOSEVELT began, his tone measured and composed. "You told me several years ago that Germany would declare war soon after the Japanese attacked."

"Indeed, I did," Mr. Mason confirmed, standing before the President with a sense of acknowledgment.

"Yet here we are. Japan is surrendering, yet Germany is neutral. The same applies to Italy."

"Yes, Mr. President, I understand. I'll admit, I'm not entirely sure why they didn't declare war yet. All the records, everything indicated that this is what would have happened."

"And yet it didn't," Roosevelt said methodically and slowly, his brows furrowing in contemplation.

"Admittedly, things have not gone quite to plan," Mr. Mason offered in an attempt to defend himself.

"That's an understatement," Roosevelt snapped. "You told me what the Germans are doing, what they are planning. They now know what we can do. They are planning something, and we have no idea what it is!"

Mr. Mason took in a deep breath and sighed. "This is my fault, and I take full responsibility. Senator Truman once said 'the buck stops here,' and I intend to live by that."

"Huh, that's a good saying," Roosevelt admitted. "Still, we need to know what is going to happen. If you don't, then there is little point in further conversation."

"I understand," Mr. Mason conceded. "Still, I want to help where I can."

Roosevelt nodded. "Thank you, and I will gladly accept any further help you can give, but not quite at the rate it was before."

Suddenly, Roosevelt's phone rang, breaking the charged atmosphere. He wasn't expecting any calls, and he answered it cautiously.

"Hello."

"Mr. President, Secretary Stimson needs to speak to you urgently."

Without warning, the door to the Oval Office burst open, revealing an exasperated Henry Stimson, Secretary of War. He looked disheveled, as if he had just returned from a run, and was breathing heavily.

"Secretary Stimson, what seems to be the issue?" Roosevelt asked, sensing the urgency in the air.

Even before Stimson could speak, Mr. Mason knew that whatever it was, it was bad. Really bad.

"It's the Germans," Stimson stuttered. "They... They have attacked New York City."

"My God," Roosevelt said, his expression turning grave. "What... What did they do?"

"It was an air raid, somehow launched from Germany. Downtown Manhattan has been destroyed."

Roosevelt turned to Mr. Mason, his mouth agape. "Do you have any idea what could cause this?"

"I, I... Uhhhh." Suddenly, an idea surfaced in Mr. Mason's mind. "Yes, yes, I think I do know what did this. But all our uhhh... intelligence indicated it was not ready based on what Germany had available."

"What is it, Fred?" Roosevelt pressed, his eyes narrowing with a sense of foreboding.

"It's called the Amerikabomber."

FREDRICK'S MASON'S theory was proved correct only an hour later, when Germany made a radio broadcast, describing what they did, and declaring war of the United States for the atomic bombings of Japan. Hitler personally made the search declaring this in front of the entire Reichstag. This was soon confirmed by a letter delivered by the German chancellor:

DECLARATION OF WAR

Reichstag, Berlin - May 8, 1942

To the United States of America and President Franklin D. Roosevelt,

THE TWO PRESIDENTS

In light of recent events that have shaken the foundations of global stability, it is with grave determination that the Greater German Reich must address the perilous actions undertaken by the United States, actions that have left an indelible mark on the course of history.

The unwarranted and callous bombings of Hiroshima and Tokyo, conducted by American forces utilizing atomic weapons, stand as a blatant disregard for the principles of humanity and international order. The wanton destruction and loss of civilian lives demand accountability and justice. The heinous act perpetrated against the Japanese people, an ally to the Axis powers, cannot be left unanswered.

Moreover, recent developments have thrust upon us the realization that our great nation is no longer immune to the threats posed by those who claim to champion freedom and democracy. The unprovoked attack on the heart of Germania, conducted through an air raid on New York City, is an affront to the sovereignty and dignity of the Greater German Reich.

In response to these acts of aggression, and with a solemn duty to safeguard the well-being of our people, the Reichstag, acting under the authority of the Führer, hereby declares a state of war between the Greater German Reich and the United States of America.

This declaration is not made lightly, but in the face of an enemy that has displayed a callous disregard for the sanctity of life and the principles of international law. The actions of the United States demand a resolute response, and we, the people of the Greater German Reich, stand united in defense of our ideals and the security of our homeland.

May this declaration serve as a testament to the resolve of the German people, and may history judge our actions with the fairness and clarity they deserve.

Signed,
Adolf Hitler, Führer of the Greater German Reich

FRANKLIN ROOSEVELT had seen his fervent desire fulfilled—a war with Germany. However, the victory was stained with the crimson of Manhattan's streets, where the toll on human lives far surpassed that fateful day at Pearl Harbor. The casualties, predominantly civilians, left an indelible mark on the nation. Iconic buildings stood as mere remnants of their former grandeur, and the Statue of Liberty, a symbol of freedom, lay battered and half-sunken in the harbor, barely clinging to Liberty Island.

The chaos that ensued, the magnitude of injuries sustained, was nothing short of staggering. It was a stark reckoning, reminiscent of the surprise blow America had been dealt Japan at Pearl Harbor, now reciprocated by a relentless German assault on New York City. The city that never sleeps was now thrust into a harrowing state of disarray, its citizens reeling from the aftermath of an unexpected and devastating attack.

President Roosevelt, just one day after the tragedy, stood once more before a hastily assembled Congress. The gravity of the situation etched deep lines of concern on his face as he sought the collective strength of the nation in the face of this new and formidable adversary. The echoes of his previous declarations still lingered in the hallowed halls, but now, the urgency and somber tone had intensified.

"Members of Congress, my fellow Americans," Roosevelt began, his voice resonating with a blend of resolve and sorrow. "Yesterday, our great nation faced an unprecedented assault. The heart of our democracy, the very soul of our liberty, was targeted in an act of aggression that has left us wounded and mourning."

He recounted the devastation, the loss of life, and the profound impact on the city that stood as a testament to American resilience. "In the wake of this tragedy, we find ourselves once again at a crossroads. The Germans have reached across the vast expanse of the Atlantic to strike at our homeland, and we must respond with unwavering resolve."

Asking once more for a declaration of war, Roosevelt spoke of the sacrifices that lay ahead, the challenges that awaited, and the need for unity in the face of adversity. The American people, having felt the anguish of an unexpected and brutal assault, were now called upon to rise again, to confront an enemy that had dared to shatter the tranquility of their own shores.

The path ahead was uncertain, the cost immeasurable, but the beacon of liberty that had guided the nation through its darkest hours still flickered in the resolve of its people. Roosevelt, the commander-in-chief, sought not only a declaration of war but an unwavering commitment to defend the principles upon which the United States of America was built.

As he concluded his address, he looked out over the assembly, his eyes reflecting a mix of determination and grief. The world had changed once again, and the nation stood poised at the precipice of a new chapter—one that would test the mettle of a nation, its leaders, and its citizens.

Chapter 5

Mr. Mason

THE WHITE HOUSE, WASHINGTON D.C, 2045

President Fredrick Mason, an unexpected occupant of the highest office in the land, had become a reluctant maestro in orchestrating the nation through the cacophony of global conflict. A history professor by vocation, he now found himself navigating the tumultuous waters of a world at war.

The scale of the conflict was unparalleled, a total war that spanned the globe. NATO and its allies clashed fiercely against a formidable alliance comprising Russia, Iran, India, and China. The alliances, forged through geopolitical intricacies and historical commitments, dragged nations into the fray, some regretting their predetermined roles.

The weight of leadership pressed heavily upon President Mason as he scrutinized a map, tracing the ominous dance of troop movements. The recent invasion of northern Canada and Alaska, a surprise offensive through the North Pole, had set an alarming tone. Simultaneously, the second invasion of Ukraine lingered in a perpetual stalemate, while the fortresses of Iran and China presented insurmountable challenges. The unfolding chaos seemed to defy resolution.

Amidst this geopolitical maelstrom, the doors to the Oval Office burst open, admitting a procession of generals and a cohort of Secret Service agents led by Bailey, the chief security officer.

"Mr. President," Bailey's voice cut through the room's tension, "We need to get you to the PEOC now!" Urgency marked her words as she guided the president towards the secure bunker.

"Bailey, what's going on?" President Mason sought clarity amidst the chaos.

"Several enemy aircraft were spotted circling D.C. at a high altitude," she explained tersely.

"A secret weapon of mass destruction, we suspect," one of the generals added, the gravity of the situation evident in his expression.

"A secret weapon?" President Mason questioned, the surreal nature of the threat fueling his concern. "What kind of weapon necessitates such an ominous circling?"

"We don't know," the general admitted, mirroring the collective uncertainty shrouding the room.

In the tense descent to the PEOC, the subterranean refuge beneath the White House, a subtle vibration beneath their feet went unnoticed. President Mason, stepping into the confined space, demanded information, attempting to assert control amidst the encroaching unknowns. The world outside seemed to tremble, mirroring the uncertainty that echoed within the walls of the subterranean command center.

"What's the latest situation?" President Mason demanded, seamlessly taking control of the tense situation unfolding in the PEOC.

"Enemy aircraft seem to be creating some sort of contrail around D.C. Spotters are reporting massive amounts of lightning coming from the resulting cloud cover," a military official briefed, the urgency palpable in his voice.

President Mason furrowed his brow. "Lightning? What could they be doing?" At that very moment, he detected an intensifying vibration beneath his feet. It was an ominous sign, a prelude to something significant.

"Everyone, get down!" he yelled instinctively, prompting a flurry of movements as people scrambled to find cover. The vibrations heightened, becoming almost deafening, while the air was charged with an eerie glow. Those who failed to heed the warning began to disintegrate, leaving only their legs below the knees.

"By God, what have they done?" President Mason exclaimed in shock as he witnessed the horrifying spectacle unfold.

A blinding flash illuminated the bunker, and as suddenly as it began, the vibrations ceased, leaving an eerie silence in its wake. Only the severed legs of those who stood moments ago remained.

"Everyone stay down!" President Mason urged, a cautious vigilance enveloping the survivors. Minutes passed in silence before he attempted to rise, but Bailey, the lead Secret Service agent, intervened.

"Mr. President, let me go first," she insisted. Aware of Bailey's unwavering resolve, President Mason nodded reluctantly.

Bailey rose cautiously, confirming that whatever had disintegrated the others had dissipated. The survivors slowly emerged from the shelter, numbering about 30 or 40. President Mason pondered the inexplicable events that had just transpired.

"What had they done?" he wondered silently, noting that most of the equipment in the bunker had lost power, despite backup generators.

A sudden banging echoed outside the bunker doors, accompanied by shouting. Given the cataclysmic events, such sounds should have been impossible. The survivors hesitated, their cautious silence broken only by the distant commotion.

President Mason, deciding to take action, approached the door. "Mr. President—" Bailey began but was abruptly cut off as the door swung open. Two men in Secret Service outfits tackled President Mason to the ground, eliciting a defensive response from his own remaining security detail.

"What in the hell is going on here?" another voice demanded, recognizable to President Mason, but should have been impossible. "What is this palace?"

President Mason's eyes widened as he recognized President Franklin Roosevelt being wheeled into the bunker. The shockwave of surprise reverberated through the room, causing the armed guards to lower their weapons.

"Mr. President," one of FDR's security details began, "You shouldn't be here, we don't know—"

"I will do as I please, Mike," Roosevelt interrupted. "I would like to hear from them on how they built this secret bunker under the White House."

The two Secret Service agents, unaware of President Mason's identity, heaved him up. "Mr. President, I don't think you're going to believe me when I tell you who we are," President Mason declared matter-of-factly.

"Try me," Roosevelt replied.

Drawing on his knowledge of events, President Mason explained their origin and predicament. The survivors deduced that the enemy forces had employed an anti-matter weapon, and the cloud cover was intended to contain its effects. The occupants of the PEOC were the sole survivors of the 2045 anti-matter bombing of Washington, D.C., and inexplicably found themselves thrust back in time to the year 1933, the first term of President FDR. The realization of their predicament hung in the air as the survivors grappled with the profound implications of their unexpected journey through time.

SIGHING WITH A SENSE of resignation, Frederick Mason arrived at an unassuming home nestled in a quiet residential corner of Washington, D.C. The journey from the bunker had been a surreal transition, leaving behind the clandestine existence beneath the White House for a life reshaped by the unpredictable currents of time.

Once it became clear that none of the bunker's occupants had any records and with no better explanation for the sudden appearance of the PEOC, President Roosevelt swiftly embraced their extraordinary story. Recognizing Mason's unique experience—albeit only a few months more in presidential terms—Roosevelt extended an offer for him to serve as a special advisor. Grateful for the camaraderie, Mason accepted, stepping into a role that melded past and present.

Under Roosevelt's guidance, arrangements were made to provide housing for the survivors. In a collective effort to recreate elements of their former lives, the enclave was born—a hub where reproductions of 2045 technology and lifestyles coexisted with the atmosphere of 1933.

The survivors, united by the shared tragedy of losing their families in the bombing, sought solace and new connections within the enclave. Bonds forged in grief transformed into relationships, a unique camaraderie forming among those who alone understood the weight of their shared history.

For Frederick Mason, the mantle of the presidency had shifted to Roosevelt, and with it came a freedom he hadn't experienced since before the bombing. No longer in need of a secret service detail when his identity remained shrouded in the annals of history, Mason found himself unburdened by the trappings of his former office. However, Bailey, the steadfast and skeptical Secret Service agent, remained by his side, her loyalty evolving into something deeper.

In 1936, Frederick Mason and Bailey exchanged vows, uniting their lives against the backdrop of a world trying to rewrite its future. As a trusted advisor, Mason shared insights and warnings with FDR, offering a glimpse into the unfolding events in Europe. Plans were set in motion based on this future knowledge, a bold attempt to shape a better outcome. Yet, in the shadow of the devastating bombing of Manhattan, it appeared their efforts had fallen short.

Entering their home, Mason found Bailey tuned in to the radio, her eyes focused on any updates regarding the bombing. She wore her Secret Service uniform, something he hadn't seen her wear in almost six years.

"Hey, I take it you heard the news?" Frederick said to his wife, Bailey, grabbing her hands as he did so.

"Yeah, I heard the news," she replied sharply. "It's kind of hard to miss."

"Yeah," he said before sitting down, placing his head in his hands. "I think I might have done the wrong thing."

Bailey looked at Frederick and walked over to him. "You did what you thought was the right thing. You had a tough choice to make, and you made it, like a president."

"Yeah, yeah, I mean...." She kissed Frederick deeply on the lips.

"Sorry," she said, pulling back. "Considering what just happened in New York, that seemed inappropriate."

"No, it's fine. I'd like to consider it as if we were flipping off Hitler and his tactics."

Bailey smiled sweetly.

"Franklin and I are heading to New York to assess the damage next week," Frederick said bluntly.

"Hmmm, sounds like you'll need protection. I could get the gang back together again."

"It's the 1940s; people will notice if you're a Secret Service agent."

"Ehhhh, maybe I'll become the new Rosie the Riveter."

Frederick laughed, and soon Bailey joined in. "I would like that, I think."

"Good," she said, smiling once again. "Because you have no choice in the matter."

"Yes, dear," Frederick said.

The two finished up for the day, engaging in a playful exchange of ideas about what could happen if they shared certain information with Roosevelt. They soon formulated a clear plan for their next steps, aligning themselves with the uncertain future that awaited them.

TOURING THE REMNANTS of downtown Manhattan proved to be an overwhelming experience for Mr. Mason, who struggled to conceal the emotions threatening to surface. The devastation mirrored haunting images of New York City post-9/11, a tragedy he had only seen in photographs given his birth date, and the stark resemblance sent shivers down his spine.

Though he attempted to compose himself, Mr. Mason couldn't escape the crushing weight of responsibility. His advice had set in motion a chain reaction that culminated in this catastrophic event. The destruction, the sorrow, all bore the imprint of his choices, making him directly accountable. Taking a deep breath, he fought to regain control, realizing that Roosevelt, too, was grappling with the same anguish.

As Frederick maneuvered his way through the rubble, he observed Roosevelt, tears streaming down the president's face. Refusing assistance, Roosevelt defiantly navigated the destruction, openly using his wheelchair to spite the press rather than as a concession to his physical limitations.

Anti-aircraft nests were scattered amid the wreckage, manned by soldiers hungry for revenge against the Germans. Trigger-happy and fueled by a desperate need for retribution, they dared any German bomber to appear during this visit.

"My God," Roosevelt uttered, his voice barely audible as he surveyed the unimaginable damage. The president seemed on the verge of openly weeping, the weight of the tragedy bearing heavily on his shoulders.

Amid the debris, body parts protruded, left unattended as grim reminders of lives lost. As they approached a collapsed building, the grim reality became even starker—the small bodies of children lay among the ruins, innocent lives senselessly taken.

Anger coursed through Mr. Mason, a seething resentment toward Hitler for the heinous orders that had led to such devastation. The desire to witness justice for the perpetrators intensified, and even Mr. Mason, who had once stood against the death penalty, found himself questioning his convictions, especially when dealing with literal Nazis.

In somber silence, the group, including other advisors and government officials, continued their tour. Words seemed inadequate in the face of the profound loss and collective grief that engulfed them. The weight of responsibility hung heavily in the air, their right to speak now overshadowed by the gravity of the consequences they were witnessing.

Chapter 6

Into the Wild Blue Yonder

TWO WEEKS LATER...

Army Air Force Captain William Anderson was a man fueled by determination, his resolve hardened by a deep-seated need for revenge in the aftermath of the New York tragedy. While he had initially enlisted after the attack on Pearl Harbor with the intent to fight against the Japanese, their relatively swift surrender left him with a lingering sense of unfulfilled vengeance. It was the Germans, in their despicable actions, who had become the focus of his wrath.

Currently soaring over Dresden, Germany, Captain Anderson's aircraft bore a single payload—one atomic bomb. The decision to drop such a weapon was fraught with peril, but in his mind, it was a risk worth taking. However, this was far from a sanctioned mission; he was acting on his own accord.

"This will teach them," he thought resolutely, the silence within the cockpit accentuating the hum of the aircraft's engines as the only audible companion. Isolated and left to his own devices, he would have to navigate the complexities of deploying the atomic bomb independently.

The monotonous hum was abruptly shattered by the thunderous sound of explosions echoing around him. The Germans had detected his presence, and the once serene flight now morphed into a chaotic ballet of evasion.

Reacting swiftly, Captain Anderson initiated evasive maneuvers, skillfully navigating the skies in an attempt to evade the incoming fire. In this moment, the gravity of his self-imposed mission weighed heavily on him. Doubt crept in, questioning the sanity of his decision. "Why did he think this was a good idea?" echoed in his mind as he grappled with the escalating danger.

Suddenly, the aircraft lurched violently to the side. Glancing back, Captain Anderson's heart sank as he realized his wing was gone. Panic and regret flooded his senses as the reality of his situation became unmistakable.

"Fuck, Bill, you've fucked up," he screamed into the solitude of the cockpit, the descent of his crippled aircraft accelerating rapidly, hurtling toward an uncertain fate.

THE CHAOTIC AFTERMATH of the downed aircraft was swiftly infiltrated by SS soldiers, their stoic demeanor unyielding even in the face of the acrid scent of burning fuel and twisted wreckage. Methodically sifting through the debris, their hands worked with practiced efficiency to extract the lifeless body of the lone pilot. The solemn task, routine for them, hinted at the inherent brutality of their occupation, and they would later commit the pilot to a makeshift grave.

What perplexed the SS soldiers, however, was the glaring anomaly of the solitary plane. It defied the established modus operandi of the Allies. Questions lingered in the air—what were they thinking, and why was this aircraft flying alone?

In the midst of this perplexity, a young recruit's urgent shouts pierced the uneasy silence. His distress emanated from the vicinity of what seemed to have once been the bomb bay. Reacting to his call for assistance, several SS men hastened to his side, their eyes widening as they took in the revelation before them.

As the gravity of the discovery unfolded, a series of swift orders in German resonated through the air. The situation had escalated beyond the purview of routine procedures; the involvement of the Gestapo, the notorious secret police, was deemed imperative. The unexpected circumstances had set in motion a chain of events that would unravel a complex web of intrigue and intensify the scrutiny of the enigmatic situation at hand.

PRESIDENT FRANKLIN Roosevelt found himself engulfed in the depths of a harrowing day. The theft of an atomic bomb, coupled with the hijacking of a bomber flown deep into enemy territory, marked a catastrophic turn of events, the severity of which surpassed anything the president had faced before. The grim reality loomed large – the Germans likely had possession of the atomic bomb, and the disconcerting prospect of their potential reverse engineering efforts intensified the gravity of the situation.

Summoning Mr. Mason seemed futile to Roosevelt in this unprecedented crisis. Doubtful that any advice could navigate the uncharted waters of such a calamity, Roosevelt resigned himself to the grim task of untangling the complexities alone. Setting his pen aside, he pressed his hands into his temples, attempting to ward off the insistent headache that accompanied the tumultuous events unfolding.

The weight of the situation bore down on Roosevelt's shoulders, leaving him in a mental quagmire as he grappled with the implications. He could barely focus amid the chaos, and the question that lingered in his mind was not only what had happened but, more significantly, what would happen next. The uncertainty of the future loomed ominously, and Roosevelt faced the daunting challenge of steering the nation through uncharted territory, desperately seeking solutions within the confines of his troubled thoughts.

ADOLF HITLER FOUND himself unexpectedly elated as he perused the daily report from his advisors. The revelation that the American atom bomb had been successfully captured, fully intact, from a lone downed bombardier brought a surge of triumph to the notoriously stern visage of the dictator. Puzzled by the audacity of the American plan to venture into German airspace without air superiority, Hitler couldn't deny the potential game-changing implications of this acquisition. If confirmed functional, this newfound weapon promised to tip the scales of the war effort significantly in Germany's favor.

In a rare display of emotion, the Führer allowed a smile to grace his face. This triumph, in his eyes, was more than a strategic victory; it was a manifestation of German superiority. The mere possession of the American atom bomb served as a potent symbol of dominance. In his conviction, Hitler believed that the Americans were about to experience a reality-altering revelation, one that would underscore Germany's unrivaled strength.

A chuckle escaped Hitler's lips as he contemplated the unfolding scenario. Rising from his desk, he decided to indulge in some personal time with Eva. Today, he believed, marked the beginning of a profound transformation. The captured atom bomb had become the catalyst for a new chapter in the war, one that held the promise of reshaping the course of history in favor of the Axis powers.

FREDRICK MASON SAT in stunned silence, his hands tightly gripping the glass containing a drink that now seemed more bitter than ever. The unimaginable had happened – Nazi Germany possessed the atomic bomb, a disastrous outcome he himself had advocated for in the past. Regret and guilt washed over him, and he couldn't escape the weight of his own decisions.

Bailey approached her husband, her steps echoing a mixture of sympathy and concern. She could sense the turmoil within Fredrick as he grappled with the consequences of his actions.

"I take it it's still bothering you," she said gently, her voice a soothing presence behind him.

Fredrick could only manage a nod, his gaze fixed on the drink that symbolized the destructive power he had unleashed upon the world.

"Well, you need to try and move on," Bailey suggested, her eyes meeting Fredrick's in an attempt to convey reassurance.

His response was a despondent admission, "Yeah."

Bailey, resolute and direct, continued, "We've all had to do that since we arrived here."

"I... I can't do that. It's all my fault," Fredrick confessed, the weight of culpability heavy in his words. "My actions caused the early development of the bomb. It caused Germany to develop the Amerikabomber instead of developing the V2. I've made a mess of history and have given Adolf Hitler the means of taking over the world."

"No, you didn't," Bailey asserted, cutting through his self-condemnation.

"What?" Fredrick replied, taken aback by her blunt response.

"Us being sent back in time already messed up history. That wasn't your fault; the war wasn't your fault. You did what you thought was right and attempted to make a better world," Bailey explained, her words laced with a pragmatic wisdom.

"But—"

"No buts," Bailey declared sternly. "All you can do is make the best decision at the time, and you did that. That is all you can do, what anyone can do. You can only make the best of the situation at hand."

"I don't know how," Fredrick bemoaned, feeling lost in the chaos of his own making.

"Yes, you do," Bailey encouraged. "You were elected president after all. I know it's been a while, but you need to put on your President Mason hat for a while and make the best of the situation."

Bailey smiled, reaching out to hold Fredrick's hands in a gesture of support. He managed a faint smile in return, appreciating the strength she provided in a moment of weakness.

"Yes, of course. You always know what to say."

"I know," Bailey replied, offering a quick but tender kiss on Fredrick's lips before pulling away, leaving him with a renewed sense of purpose and a glimmer of hope amid the shadows of uncertainty.

As Bailey withdrew from the brief but comforting exchange, the atmosphere hung heavy with the gravity of the situation. Fredrick, still grappling with the enormity of his role in altering the course of history, felt a renewed surge of determination fueled by Bailey's unwavering support.

In the quietude that followed, Bailey's gaze remained fixed on Fredrick, her eyes reflecting a mix of compassion and confidence. She recognized that her husband, burdened by the consequences of his decisions, needed more than just words of reassurance. It was time to awaken the leader within him, the President Mason who had once steered the nation through turbulent times.

"You're not alone in this, Fredrick," Bailey said, her voice carrying a gentle yet firm conviction. "We've been given a chance to set things right, and together, we'll find a way."

Fredrick nodded, absorbing the strength in her words. The weight on his shoulders seemed to shift as he drew upon the reservoirs of resilience that had propelled him into leadership before.

Bailey continued, "Remember why you were elected president. Your ability to navigate crises, to make tough decisions for the greater good – those qualities haven't disappeared. They are part of who you are, and now, more than ever, the world needs someone with your vision and leadership."

As the gravity of his past actions began to transform into a catalyst for redemption, Fredrick slowly stood up. He looked into Bailey's eyes, recognizing the unwavering belief she held in him. The room, once filled with a sense of despair, now resonated with the possibility of forging a new path.

"I know it's a daunting task," Bailey admitted, "but history has a way of providing opportunities for redemption. You have the chance to shape a different future, one where the mistakes of the past are acknowledged, learned from, and rectified."

A sense of purpose flickered in Fredrick's eyes. The weight of guilt began to lift, replaced by a determination to confront the challenges ahead. Bailey squeezed his hand, offering silent encouragement.

"You're not alone, Fredrick. We're in this together," she affirmed.

With Bailey's support and the echoes of his own leadership echoing in his mind, Fredrick Mason stepped forward, ready to face the consequences of his actions and forge a new destiny for a world on the brink of chaos. The road ahead was uncertain, but with each step, they carried the hope of a better tomorrow.

In a moment of revelation, a surge of inspiration electrified Fredrick Mason's thoughts, offering a glimmer of hope amidst the turmoil. An idea, bold and potentially transformative, sprang to life in his mind – one that could salvage the dire situation they now faced.

"I need to get to the White House right now," Fredrick declared, the urgency evident in his voice as he propelled himself upward from his chair.

The sudden determination in his eyes didn't escape Bailey's notice. She looked at him with a mixture of pride and understanding. "I knew you had it in you," she said, a supportive smile gracing her lips.

Fredrick acknowledged her with a grateful nod. "All thanks to you." With those words, he leaned in and pressed a fervent kiss onto Bailey's lips, a momentary exchange of shared strength and unwavering support.

As the kiss concluded, Fredrick wasted no time. He hastily grabbed his coat, the fabric rustling with the urgency of his mission, and headed for the door. The gravity of his purpose hung in the air, a weight matched only by the determination etched across his face.

The door swung open, and Fredrick stepped out into the brisk air. The world outside seemed to be in a state of suspended animation, unaware of the seismic decisions brewing within the mind of the man now striding purposefully through the quiet streets.

Chapter 7

The Future lends a hand

PRESIDENT FRANKLIN Roosevelt leaned forward, his expression a mix of contemplation and concern, as his most trusted advisor, Fred Mason, laid out a plan to address the escalating issue with Germany. The intricacies of the proposal hung in the air, acknowledged by Roosevelt as effective yet undeniably fraught with risks that cast a shadow over the room.

"Fred, are you sure this is the only way?" Roosevelt queried, his curiosity evident.

"I am certain, Mr. President," emphasized Mr. Mason. "Recent events have accelerated the German war machine beyond what was originally anticipated. Utilizing the 2045 technology wouldn't just level the playing field; it would utterly annihilate it."

Roosevelt, ever cautious, considered the implications. "Yes, I understand. Still, if the Krauts get their hands on these weapons—"

"We are doomed. Yes, I get that," Mr. Mason finished for the president. "But given the rapid advancements they've made, we have little choice if we want the timeline to maintain some semblance of its original course."

"I think it's too late for that," Roosevelt mused.

"Yeah, I know that too," Mr. Mason concurred. "I'm already worried that we will have desensitized the nation to the use of nuclear weapons."

Roosevelt, stroking his chin, contemplated the consequences. "That wouldn't be conducive at all."

"Still, we can't do much about it," Mr. Mason shrugged. "I feel we have little choice but to pursue these options."

Roosevelt sighed, acknowledging the grim reality. "I don't like it, but I agree. Prepare me a list of what you think would be useful and who you can trust with this information. I believe it's best to keep time travels as low-key as possible."

"Understood," Mr. Mason affirmed. "I will get right on those lists."

"See that you do," Roosevelt directed. "That is all."

With those words, Mr. Mason turned and left for a makeshift room that had become his impromptu office. The weight of responsibility hung heavy on his shoulders as he faced the monumental task ahead. The dim light in the room seemed to echo the gravity of the decisions to be made, and as Mr. Mason immersed himself in his duties, he knew that time was of the essence. There was much to do, and the fate of the world hung in the balance.

WERNHER VON BRAUN STOOD in disbelief, facing the man who had set the course of his life on an entirely unforeseen trajectory all those years ago. Mr. Mason, a time traveler from the future, had handpicked him, steering Von Braun's destiny in a direction unknown even to the brilliant scientist. The enigma of his original fate loomed, shrouded in Mr. Mason's deliberate secrecy.

Von Braun, grappling with the revelation, took a deep breath, trying to comprehend the magnitude of the situation. His existence was not a product of random chance; he was a chosen participant in a grander scheme. The uncertainty of what could have been haunted him, but as Mr. Mason had emphasized, the present circumstances demanded his attention.

"So," Von Braun began slowly, "Why me? Why are you telling me this?"

"I'm telling you because I trust you, Wernher," Mr. Mason responded genuinely. "I need your help integrating 2045 technology into a fighter."

Von Braun's mind wrestled with conflicting emotions. To use advanced technology against his native land, the country he once called home, raised a moral dilemma that he couldn't easily dismiss.

"To use against a country I called home for most of my life," Von Braun pondered aloud.

"Unfortunately yes," Mr. Mason replied bluntly.

"...and one that you manipulated into a war with my new home," Von Braun continued, probing the uncomfortable truth.

"Also yes," Mr. Mason admitted shamefully. "Though not in the way it was done. Not at all like... like this."

The weight of the revelation hung heavily in the room, the air thick with unspoken tension. Von Braun broke the silence with a single word, "O.K."

Mr. Mason, visibly relieved, responded with eagerness, "Really?"

"Yes," Von Braun affirmed. "America is my home now, and I doubt I can set foot in Germany. If I can help liberate the people of Germany and bring an end to this war, then I will take it."

Mr. Mason, touched by the genuine commitment, realized that Von Braun's German accent had started to falter, a testament to the complexity of emotions that tugged at the scientist's loyalty.

"Thank you, Dr. Von Braun. You don't know what this means to me," Mr. Mason said, extending his hand for a shake.

"Yes, well, I suppose I have some work to do," Von Braun said, opting not to shake hands. "Are you going to give me a list of what future technology you have access to?"

"Oh, yes... of course," Mr. Mason replied, slightly flustered.

As the conversation shifted to the practicalities of their collaboration, Mr. Mason, with a mix of excitement and anxiety, began detailing the future technologies at their disposal. The once-unthinkable alliance between a time traveler and a brilliant scientist was forged, as they embarked on a mission to create a formidable force that would defy the expectations of both history and Adolf Hitler. Together, they would design a weapon that would reshape the course of the war and, perhaps, alter the destiny of nations.

Subject: Urgent Military Report - German Atomic Bombing of Boston and Reverse-Engineered Stolen U.S. Nuclear Technology

Date: August 15, 1942

To: President Franklin D. Roosevelt

From: General Marshall, U.S. Army

Mr. President,

I regret to inform you of a grave development that has unfolded in the ongoing conflict with Germany. In a shocking turn of events, the city of Boston was targeted and subsequently struck by a German atomic bomb delivered via the notorious Amerikabomber. This event occurred on August 10, 1942, resulting in catastrophic consequences for the city and its inhabitants.

Details of the Attack:

On the aforementioned date, at approximately 0800 hours, our radar systems detected an unidentified aircraft approaching the northeastern coast of the United States. Unfortunately, due to the stealth capabilities of the Amerikabomber, it successfully evaded our early warning systems until it was too late to mount a defense.

At 0905 hours, the enemy aircraft released an atomic bomb over the city of Boston, resulting in a devastating explosion. Preliminary estimates suggest extensive casualties and severe infrastructural damage. We are currently mobilizing rescue and relief efforts, but the scale of the disaster is unprecedented.

Enemy Capability:

Intelligence reports indicate that the Germans have achieved a significant technological breakthrough in nuclear weapons development. The Amerikabomber, equipped with an atomic bomb, demonstrates their capability to strike major U.S. cities with devastating precision. The magnitude of this threat cannot be overstated, and immediate action is imperative.

Reverse-Engineered U.S. Nuclear Technology:

Disturbingly, our worst fears have been confirmed, with evidence that the German forces have successfully reverse-engineered the stolen U.S. nuclear device from the May incident. The implications of this are alarming, as it suggests a breach in our security protocols and the potential for further devastating attacks on American soil.

Recommendations:

1. Military Mobilization: Immediate deployment of military resources to secure vulnerable cities and critical infrastructure against potential follow-up attacks.

2. Enhanced Intelligence and Counterintelligence: Strengthen intelligence efforts to identify and neutralize enemy operatives responsible for the theft of U.S. nuclear technology. Implement heightened security measures across our research facilities.

3. International Cooperation: Engage with our Allied nations to share intelligence and collaborate on strategies to counter the German nuclear threat. Seek support for joint military operations against German nuclear facilities.

4. Civil Defense Measures: Implement stringent civil defense measures in major cities to minimize civilian casualties and facilitate efficient evacuation procedures in the event of future attacks.

Mr. President, the situation is dire, and immediate action is crucial to safeguard the nation. Our military and intelligence communities stand ready to execute your directives in this critical time.

Respectfully,

George C. Marshall

General, U.S. Army

Joint Chiefs of Staff

PRESIDENT FRANKLIN Roosevelt trembled with a mixture of anger, sorrow, and regret as he grappled with the news of yet another devastating attack on American soil. The destructive force of the German atomic bomb had obliterated Boston, leaving a once-thriving city reduced to ruins and millions of lives shattered. The weight of the decision to authorize the construction of such a destructive weapon now bore down on him with an unbearable intensity. He wished he had never authored the creation of that infernal device.

As the reality of the situation sank in, Roosevelt found himself acknowledging the grim truth – Fredrick's plan, once viewed with skepticism, was now the only viable option to counter the German threat. The time for alternative strategies had passed; the urgency of the moment demanded a response that matched the ruthlessness of their adversary.

Roosevelt's phone jolted him from his somber contemplation, and he swiftly picked it up, a sense of foreboding lingering in the air.

"Hello," he answered, his voice carrying the burden of the decisions he had made.

"Mr. President," General Marshall's voice echoed through the receiver.

"General," Roosevelt acknowledged, bracing himself for more distressing news.

"We just got word. The Germans have struck again."

"Dear Lord," Roosevelt uttered, his mind racing with the magnitude of the unfolding crisis. His thoughts immediately turned to the devastation wrought upon another unsuspecting city. "Where?"

"Alaska."

"Alaska," Roosevelt repeated, momentarily perplexed. The revelation left him searching for a motive behind this particular target. Then, it dawned on him – New Jerusalem, the settlement he had authorized at the behest of Mr. Mason to provide a haven for Jewish refugees from war-torn Europe.

"Gone, sir," General Marshall confirmed.

Roosevelt's heart sank. This was not a military installation nor a strategic target; it was a community of displaced and vulnerable people seeking refuge. The attack on New Jerusalem transcended the boundaries of war strategy; it was a heinous war crime.

Chapter 8

German Jubilee

ADOLF HITLER REVELED in a sinister satisfaction as he perused the latest report, a testament to the success of his meticulously devised plans. The Amerikabomber, the pinnacle of German technological ingenuity, had achieved unprecedented reach in its recent mission, striking fear into the heart of the enemy. The grin that adorned Hitler's face hinted at the proximity of his ultimate goal – the eradication of the Jewish race.

The recent triumphs, particularly the devastating blows delivered to Japan, fueled Hitler's confidence that victory was within reach. He envisioned a future where a few more strategic hits on American soil would force submission, leaving the British to wither away. The Soviets, a lingering concern, seemed less formidable in the face of his newfound technological prowess. The pieces of the puzzle were falling into place, paving the way for the Aryan race to ascend and dominate not only Europe but the entire world.

In the midst of Hitler's triumphant musings, an unexpected interruption rattled him – a ringing phone. His orders to avoid interruptions under any circumstance had been defied, and a sense of foreboding crept over him as he cautiously picked up the receiver.

"Gutten Tag," he grumbled into the phone, his voice laced with irritation and uncertainty.

"Mein Führer, this is Field Marshal Von Manstein," came the composed voice on the other end.

"Yes," Hitler responded coldly. "This better be important to defy my direct orders."

"I apologize, Mein Führer, but I believe this is worth your time."

"Go on...," Hitler commanded, his curiosity piqued.

"Mein Führer," Von Manstein declared confidently, "we have captured Stalin. He wishes to surrender the Soviet Union."

The news hit Hitler with unexpected force, momentarily silencing the megalomaniacal dictator. It took a few minutes for him to collect himself and respond. "Oh," he finally managed, surprised by the sudden turn of events. "I understand, Field Marshal. You have my authorization to negotiate on behalf of the Reich."

"Thank you, Mein Führer. Heil Hitler!"

"Yes, yes, Heil," Hitler replied dismissively before abruptly hanging up the phone. The news of Stalin's surrender marked yet another stride toward global dominance. Victory was seemingly within reach, and Hitler reveled in the intoxicating taste of triumph. The world, he believed, was poised to bow before the might of the Third Reich.

Surrender of the Soviet Union: A Pivotal Moment in History Unfolds in Moscow
By Anthony Bridger
November 11, 1942

THE TWO PRESIDENTS

In an unexpected turn of events that has sent shockwaves across the geopolitical landscape, the Soviet Union has officially surrendered to the forces of Nazi Germany, marking a significant chapter in the ongoing global conflict. Field Marshal Von Manstein, leading the German forces, successfully captured Soviet Premier Joseph Stalin, prompting the surrender of the once-formidable Soviet military apparatus.

The announcement came from the Reich Chancellery in Berlin, where Adolf Hitler, the architect of the Third Reich, expressed his satisfaction with the turn of events. Von Manstein, the key orchestrator of the Soviet Union's capitulation, was granted authority to negotiate the terms of surrender on behalf of the Nazi regime.

The surrender ceremony is scheduled to take place in the iconic Red Square in Moscow, a venue that has witnessed countless historic events. In a symbolic gesture, the Soviet flag is slated to be lowered as the Nazi flag is raised during the ceremony. This unprecedented act is set to be attended by Adolf Hitler himself, underscoring the gravity of the moment and the strategic importance of the Soviet surrender to the Nazi war machine.

The international community, already reeling from the recent string of German successes, is closely monitoring this development. The capitulation of the Soviet Union, a formidable military power and a key Allied force, reshapes the dynamics of the global conflict and raises critical questions about the future of Europe and beyond.

The surrender ceremony, to be held within the week, is expected to be a meticulously orchestrated affair. It will feature military parades, speeches, and the symbolic lowering of the Soviet flag alongside the Nazi flag in a move intended to assert German dominance over the conquered territory.

This development has sparked a wave of concern among Allied nations, with leaders scrambling to assess the implications of the Soviet surrender. The ripple effects of this surrender are likely to reverberate across the already tumultuous global stage, introducing new uncertainties and challenges for the Allies in their quest to thwart the expansionist ambitions of Nazi Germany.

As the world awaits the outcome of this pivotal ceremony, historians and political analysts are left grappling with the profound changes unfolding in real-time. The surrender of the Soviet Union to Nazi Germany is a stark reminder of the fragility of alliances and the unpredictability that defines the landscape of global conflict.

ADOLF HITLER, HIS MIND consumed by an unsettling mix of arrogance and disdain, questioned his decision to participate in the ceremony unfolding before him in the once-proud Red Square. The bitter wind cut through his uniform, penetrating to his very core, and he recoiled at the thought of bestowing such an honor upon what he deemed an inferior race.

His gaze remained fixed, unyielding, as the Soviet flag, a symbol of resistance and defiance, descended for the last time. In its place, the flag of the German Reich ascended, an ominous emblem of triumph and the impending shadow of German dominance. Joseph Stalin, once the indomitable leader of the Soviet Union, stood shackled and forcibly made to witness the crumbling demise of his nation. To Hitler, this degradation of his adversary was a spectacle worthy of the discomfort caused by the frigid wind.

As the Reich flag fluttered defiantly at the apex of the pole, jubilant cheers erupted throughout the square. German soldiers, whether from the Wehrmacht or the feared S.S., joined in unison to celebrate the conclusion of one of the bloodiest chapters in the war. The subjugation of the Soviet Union was complete, and Hitler reveled in the intoxicating satisfaction that surged through the crowd.

Raising his hand to quell the fervor, Hitler made his way to a prepared lectern, signaling the commencement of a speech intended to further solidify the narrative of German triumph. The anticipation in the air was palpable as the crowd fell into hushed expectancy.

"Children of Germania," Hitler began, his voice resonating through the square, a symphony of malevolence and calculated charisma. "Today marks a turning point, a triumph of the Aryan spirit over the forces of Bolshevism. The Soviet Union, a once-mighty adversary, now stands vanquished before the might of the German Reich."

He paused, allowing the weight of his words to sink in, before continuing, "Our forces have proven their prowess, and the era of Soviet resistance has come to an end. We shall redirect our indomitable war machine toward new challenges. The British, standing alone, shall soon taste the bitter fruits of defeat, and thereafter, the Americans will witness the irresistible force of the German Reich."

The square echoed with the fervent applause of the indoctrinated masses, their loyalty to the Führer unwavering. Hitler, reveling in the moment, continued to deliver a speech that painted a distorted picture of victory and destiny, obscuring the harsh realities of war and conquest with a veneer of nationalist fervor. The Red Square, once a symbol of Soviet pride, now bore witness to an unsettling transformation under the looming shadow of the swastika.

PRIME MINISTER WINSTON Churchill found himself grappling with a cascade of disheartening news that seemed to shatter the foundations of Allied resilience. France had fallen, Russia had succumbed, and now the ominous threat of unrestrained German air raids loomed over the vulnerable shores of America. The once formidable alliance stood fragmented, leaving Britain as the solitary bulwark against the encroaching forces of the Third Reich.

In a somber reflection, Churchill recollected his last meeting with his majesty, a poignant inquiry that lingered in the recesses of his mind. The king had earnestly sought the Prime Minister's counsel on any conceivable terms for peace that would not only end the bloodshed but also preserve the dignity of the British people. The weight of this request pressed heavily on Churchill's shoulders as the harsh realities of the situation became increasingly undeniable.

A heavy sigh escaped Churchill's lips as he contemplated the dire circumstances. The notion of exploring avenues for peace, however inconceivable it might have seemed before, now took root in the Prime Minister's mind. The war's unrelenting toll demanded a pragmatic assessment, and Churchill acknowledged that a comprehensive evaluation of Britain's position and prospects was imperative.

A tentative knock at the door jolted Churchill out of his contemplation, and he called out, "Yes, come in."

His secretary entered, wearing a visage of concern that did not go unnoticed by Churchill. An unspoken tension hung in the air before the secretary finally broke the silence.

"Sir, it's from intelligence, sir."

Churchill's eyebrows knitted inquisitively, wondering why intelligence would be reaching out at this juncture, bypassing the conventional channels of a war cabinet meeting. Impatiently, he prodded, "Have they sent a message? Made a breakthrough of some sort?"

"Not quite, sir, no," the secretary replied nervously, her eyes betraying the gravity of the message she carried.

"Get on with it then," Churchill urged, a sense of urgency coloring his tone.

"They believe, sir," she hesitated before delivering the unsettling news, "they believe a German invasion is imminent."

"OUR INTELLIGENCE FORCES on the ground are unanimous in their assessment. A substantial buildup of German forces in the west of France, complemented by landing craft and a formidable array of several hundred aircraft, all point to an imminent invasion—a threat that looms on our doorstep and demands immediate attention," the general reported solemnly, delivering the unsettling news that cast a shadow over the room.

Churchill, his countenance reflecting the gravity of the situation, posed a crucial question to the general, seeking confirmation of the dire intelligence. "And they are certain?"

"Yes, sir," the general affirmed, his tone betraying a sense of urgency. "They are in complete agreement. Many have already requested to pull out or to seek refuge underground. I'm inclined to grant them this."

Churchill remained hunched over, absorbing the weight of the impending crisis. Slowly, deliberately, he straightened himself, steeling his resolve as he addressed everyone in the room.

"Earlier today, his majesty asked me to explore options to sue for peace—to maintain British dignity."

A collective shock rippled through the room. The specter of surrender hung in the air, casting a somber pall over the gathered individuals.

"Would you like to know what I told him?" Churchill continued, his voice resolute. "I told him that I had my doubts Hitler would accept such an agreement that would allow Britain to retain her dignity. No, the only way to do that would be to win, and this is something I am confident we can still do. Do you know why?"

Silence pervaded the room as Churchill waited for a response that did not come.

"Britain still has her empire, her colonies, and her friends. We are not the only ones in this war, and as long as we retain them, we can still win. We will defend our island, we will fight to the last man, and if we are to lose, we will continue to fight from abroad. Hitler will shed his own blood before the British give up."

The room erupted into applause, acknowledging Churchill's stirring resolve. It was a performance delivered in the crucible of uncertainty, an impromptu rallying cry meant to uplift the spirits of those who faced an unparalleled threat. Churchill, secretly hoping that someone had written down those words, allowed himself a brief moment of satisfaction.

Suddenly, a young page burst into the room, nearly out of breath. The urgency in his demeanor signaled that the latest intelligence was of utmost importance.

"Sir, the latest intel has just come in."

"Yes, get on with it."

"The Germans, they've executed Stalin."

Chapter 9

Darkness Looms

Axis Triumphs Darkened by the Demise of Stalin: Soviet Premier Executed Following Surrender
By Anthony Bridger
November 15, 1942

In the wake of the recent surrender of the Soviet Union to German forces, a new and harrowing development has cast a pall over the Eastern Front—Soviet Premier Joseph Stalin has been executed by Axis forces, further deepening the shadows of uncertainty that have enveloped the global conflict.

Just days after the capitulation of the Soviet Union, the shocking news of Stalin's execution adds a sinister layer to the unfolding narrative of the war. The circumstances surrounding his demise remain shrouded in the fog of war, as conflicting reports and hazy details emerge from the Eastern Front.

The execution of Stalin, a figure synonymous with the resolute defense against the Axis advance, sends ripples of shock and concern through the Allied nations. With the surrender of the Soviet Union still reverberating across the international stage, the loss of its iconic leader introduces a disquieting new chapter in the conflict.

Sources indicate that Stalin, once a formidable force in the defense against the Axis onslaught, fell victim to the relentless march of German military might. The execution, a calculated blow by the Axis forces, leaves the Soviet Union grappling not only with the surrender's aftermath but also with the vacuum created by the removal of its charismatic and authoritarian leader.

The news has prompted Allied leaders to reassess their strategies and consider the strategic implications of the sudden power vacuum within the Soviet leadership. Stalin's demise marks a profound loss for the Allied cause, adding an additional layer of complexity to an already intricate geopolitical landscape.

As the world absorbs this disconcerting revelation, questions abound regarding the impact on the broader Allied war effort. The timing of Stalin's execution, mere days after the surrender, raises concerns about the potential coordination between the military and political strategies of the Axis powers.

The international community now stands on edge, awaiting further details and responses from Allied leaders. The execution of Stalin serves as a stark reminder that the war's narrative is ever-evolving, with each development shaping the course of a conflict that defies predictability.

As the Allies grapple with the loss of one of their most formidable leaders, the echoes of Stalin's execution resonate across the Eastern Front and beyond. The war, already marked by its unpredictability, now confronts the Allies with new challenges and uncertainties, signaling a darker and more complex phase in the ongoing struggle against Axis dominance.

PRESIDENT ROOSEVELT slammed the paper down onto his desk, the loud thud echoing the weight of the worsening situation as time pressed forward. With each passing day, the challenges seemed insurmountable, leaving the President to hope that whatever concoction Fred and Von Braun were brewing would be the saving grace capable of turning the tide of the war, no matter how dire it became.

Furrowing his brow, Roosevelt felt the burden of age settling upon him. The demands of the war effort were taking their toll, and he yearned for a respite—a vacation or some semblance of relaxation. The Oval Office, with its weighty decisions and ceaseless challenges, had become a crucible that tested the limits of his endurance.

Suddenly, a knock resounded at the door.

"Come in," Roosevelt called out, the door swinging open to reveal Mr. Mason. "Ah, Fred, good to see you," Roosevelt greeted with a weary smile.

"Good to see you as well, though I'm not here on a social visit. I'm here to give you an update on our... special project."

Roosevelt nodded, gesturing for Mr. Mason to close the door, shutting out the prying ears. "So, you have an update, you said?"

"Yes, sir, I do. I believe the surface-to-air missiles are ready, along with the supersonic fighters. The LOW is also ready."

"You think," Roosevelt questioned, a note of skepticism in his tone.

"It's a figure of speech," Mr. Mason retorted, defending the readiness of their secret weapons. "I know it's ready."

Roosevelt stared at Mr. Mason in silence for a few moments, weighing the gravity of the situation before relenting. "Very well, I'll inform the Joint Chiefs and see what plans we can draw up using this technology."

Mr. Mason bent down, meeting Roosevelt's gaze directly. "This will change the war."

"You said the same thing about the nukes," Roosevelt replied coldly.

"I was right, wasn't I?" Mr. Mason shot back curtly.

"True," Roosevelt stated blankly. "That is all." The President picked up his paper once again, signaling the end of the conversation.

Mr. Mason turned and left the room, understanding the weight on Roosevelt's shoulders and grateful he no longer had to bear the burden of such decisions. The challenges of war leadership, once shouldered by Mr. Mason himself, were now carried by the weary President.

ALBERT EINSTEIN WALKED through the desolation of New Jerusalem, Alaska, his steps echoing amidst the charred remains left by the ruthless onslaught of the Reich. He had miraculously survived the horrific blast and ensuing fires, a testament to his resilience against the orchestrated destruction of those who sought refuge far from the reach of Hitler's tyranny. The physicist's anger simmered beneath the surface, directed not just at the brutal act of annihilation but at the entire world that had allowed such atrocities to unfold.

The expulsion from Germany and Europe, intended to be a forced migration, had escalated into a massacre in the remote corners of Alaska. The malevolent intent of the Reich had transcended mere displacement; they sought to obliterate any trace of those they considered undesirable. Einstein, standing amidst the aftermath of this atrocity, felt a burning determination to seek justice and retribution.

His initial attempt to offer his services to the U.S. government, foreseeing the inevitable war, had met with a cold rejection. The government's decision, while disheartening, became clearer as he witnessed the devastating power of the atomic bomb. The realization dawned upon him that his knowledge, however groundbreaking, came with the potential for unimaginable destruction.

Yet, Einstein refused to succumb to despair. A deep-seated need for justice propelled him forward. The source of this malevolence, the puppeteer orchestrating the carnage, had to be confronted. The one responsible for the agony of New Jerusalem had to be held accountable. As the physicist weighed his options, he fixated on the revelation that the president's advisor, Mr. Mason, had advocated for the development of the bomb. The connection between the act of mass destruction and the advisor compelled Einstein to take matters into his own hands.

Determined and resolute, Einstein set forth on a journey to confront Mr. Mason. The trail of destruction left by the Reich had ignited a fire within him, a fervor for justice that would not be extinguished. As he traversed the remnants of New Jerusalem, Alaska, Einstein embarked on a quest to bring to justice those who had unleashed the forces of devastation upon the innocent.

WINSTON CHURCHILL FELT the weight of weariness settle upon him as he concluded his meeting with Franklin Roosevelt. Another secret weapon was on the table, one that could potentially turn the tide against Germany. However, a lingering sense of distrust gnawed at Churchill. The last secret weapon promised had backfired spectacularly, finding its way into the hands of the enemy and resulting in devastating bombings on British cities. Now, on the brink of desperation, Churchill found himself reluctantly considering this new gamble.

Rising from his chair, he ambled over to his liquor cabinet, a refuge that had witnessed the burdens of war and the weight of decisions that could alter the course of history. Pouring himself a measure of brandy, Churchill sighed, contemplating the toll the war had taken on him. Resignation loomed in the shadows of his thoughts, and he entertained the idea of stepping away from the burdens of leadership once the war came to an end. The weariness ran deep, and he craved respite from the relentless demands of wartime leadership.

His contemplations were abruptly interrupted by the shrill ring of the telephone. Churchill sighed once more, placing his glass down with a heavy clink before answering the call.

"This is Churchill. They did what? No, I understand... still. Do I have the pleasure of informing his Majesty of this?" Another heavy sigh punctuated his words. "Of course I do. I understand. I will inform him right away. Thank you."

With a heavy heart, Churchill hung up the phone, the gravity of the information settling upon him. A wave of sorrow threatened to overcome him, a sentiment he vowed never to display in public. The burdens of leadership had never been more palpable.

Picking up the phone once again, he summoned his secretary. "Nel, please contact the palace and let them know I am on my way. I need to speak to his Majesty at once. The Germans have dropped a nuclear weapon on Edinburgh."

"I'M MAKING AN EXECUTIVE decision here, Winston," declared King George VI. "We need to sue for peace; the losses... they are just too high. We can't keep going on like this!" The king's voice wavered before he stopped, fixing his gaze on his prime minister, as if expecting no rebuttal.

"I have nothing to say, Your Majesty," Churchill began. "I don't disagree with you on the need for peace and that the costs are too high. However, I'm not sure the Germans would accept a peace where Britain remains independent."

The king sighed and looked down at his shoes. "Yes, unfortunately, I see where you are coming from there. Still, I don't think we have much of a choice."

"Again, I do agree, Your Majesty. But if I may?"

"Yes?" the King said, curious about Churchill's proposal.

"I have been speaking to the Americans. They seem to think they have a new weapon that will put the Germans on their knees and force their surrender."

The King raised an eyebrow. "If I recall correctly, we've been here before."

"Yes, I am aware, and again, they are asking to launch from our shores. However, the way I see it, we have little to lose while waiting for them to strike, as it seems to take the Germans a month or two to prepare a new nuclear bomb. If the weapon is successful, then we win the war. If it's not, well, it should put us in a better negotiating position."

"That must have taken a lot for you to concede that. Did it not?"

"It took quite a lot out of me," Churchill admitted.

The King stared at his prime minister for a few moments. "Very well, we'll give them a chance. Still, we should make some preparations in case this all goes badly."

"I understand, sir, and will do so at once," Churchill said before bowing.

"See to it. That is all."

With that, the King turned and left the room. Winston stood there in silence before turning and leaving himself. Franklin better deliver on his promises. The weight of the world hung in the balance, and the destiny of nations rested on the success or failure of the proposed American intervention.

Chapter 10

Light in Darkness

COLONEL MARK JACOBS, the determined pilot of the formidable *Eliza's Revenge*, scrutinized the inky darkness enveloping the night sky as he soared through the heavens. Despite the absence of visible landmarks, his seasoned expertise and reliance on cutting-edge instruments allowed him to maintain precise navigation. The desire for revenge burned within him, fueled by the devastation his sister had endured in Manhattan when the German bombs fell.

"Thirty seconds until we're over the target," called out his navigator, breaking the tense silence in the cockpit.

"Understood," replied Colonel Jacobs tersely, mentally ticking down the seconds until the estimated time of arrival. "This is for you, Eliza," he whispered under his breath, dedicating the impending mission to his sister's memory.

"Twenty seconds," the navigator announced.

"LOW is online," the bombardier reported. "Secondary systems are armed and ready."

"Ten seconds," echoed the navigator.

Colonel Jacobs took a deep breath, his gaze fixed ahead with unwavering determination. "Fire," he commanded.

"LOW is firing," the bombardier confirmed.

From the underbelly of *Eliza's Revenge*, flashes of red and green erupted—a display of technology that shouldn't have existed in the present. The crew, kept in the dark about the origins of this cutting-edge weaponry, believed it to be a top-secret military innovation. The Laser Offensive Weaponry (LOW) performed flawlessly.

Twenty thousand feet below, chaos unfolded in Hamburg, Germany. Buildings spontaneously caught fire and seemed to explode without apparent cause. Air raid sirens wailed, yet no conventional bombs were dropped. The city plunged into pandemonium as flashes of colored light illuminated the bewildered faces of its inhabitants.

Five minutes later, Oranienburg found itself engulfed in flames, the source of the devastation shrouded in mystery. Meanwhile, *Eliza's Revenge*, having executed its mission with precision, turned back towards England. Before leaving German airspace, the aircraft deployed a secondary payload on an inconspicuous factory at the town's edge—an undisclosed facility where Germany was clandestinely building its nuclear weapons. The building erupted in flames, mirroring the fate of the city it belonged to.

A substantial blow had been dealt to the German war machine, and the audacious mission remained undetected, thanks to highly advanced anti-radar systems on board the aircraft—innovations courtesy of one Mr. Mason.

ADOLF HITLER SEETHED with fury as he surveyed the desolate remains of the Oranienburg nuclear facility. The audacity of the Allies to strike at the heart of his nuclear ambitions fueled his rage. Vengeance would be exacted; they would pay dearly for this insolence.

What infuriated Hitler even more was the enigma of the mysterious fires that had engulfed the town. The destruction had been comprehensive, yet the nearby concentration camp, a symbol of his twisted ideologies, had somehow escaped the inferno. The Allies, it seemed, couldn't even grant him the satisfaction of eradicating a portion of what he deemed an "inferior race."

In the midst of his seething thoughts, a lowly aide approached Hitler with an impeccable salute, standing at attention. "Mein Führer," the aide announced, "I would like to report that we have recovered at least three intact bomb casings for the nuclear weapons from the rubble."

"I understand," responded Hitler coldly. "How long until they are ready for deployment?"

"After an inspection, the first one can be ready for tomorrow, Mein Führer. It, it is the one the American tried to drop a few months ago."

Hitler thought of this a little bit. The irony was palpable. "Good. Inform your commanding officer that, under my orders, he is to personally ensure it is ready for tomorrow. Otherwise, there will be... consequences."

The aide swallowed nervously. "Yes, Mein Führer. I will do so right away." He saluted his leader before briskly turning away to relay the urgent order.

Hitler raised his hand to his forehead, deep in thought. The setback was substantial, but he hoped that swift action on his part would rectify the situation. The looming consequences hung in the air, a testament to the relentless pursuit of his dark ambitions.

THE TWO PRESIDENTS

"OFF WE GO INTO THE wild blue yonder,

Climbing high into the sun," resonated the joyous chorus of drunken pilots celebrating ten successful missions, the elation of a much-needed morale boost permeating the room. The news had just been broadcast over the radio, and with their rotation off, the aviators were determined to revel in their well-earned respite.

"Here they come, zooming to meet our thunder,

At them, boys, give 'er the gun!"

"Down we dive, spouting our flame from under! Off with one helluva roar! We live in fame or go down in flame. Hey! Nothing'll stop the Army Air Corps!"

The spirited singing echoed through the room as the pilots basked in the euphoria of their recent successes. Rumors circulated that the new weapons would soon target Berlin, and the joyous atmosphere hadn't been this infectious since the surrender of Japan.

Suddenly, a deafening crash disrupted the revelry as a large bomb casing smashed through the roof, careening into a table before settling on its side. Some men instinctively sought cover, while others stood frozen in fear. The air raid sirens hadn't even sounded their warning.

After a tense moment of silence, a few brave souls cautiously approached the bomb, recognizing its menacing presence. One man among them, Lieutenant Karl Hopkins, stared wide-eyed at a weapon he hadn't seen in months—the very one he was supposed to have dropped on the Germans, stolen by the traitorous Anderson.

Fueled by duty, Hopkins knew he had a job to do despite the personal setback. "Everyone, get out of here now!" he shouted, urgency and authority in his voice. His fellow servicemen, finally convinced of the gravity of the situation, began evacuating the room.

Remaining behind, Lieutenant Hopkins methodically searched for hidden survivors. Finding none, he swiftly departed himself.

Later investigations revealed that the bomb had sustained extensive damage during the bombing of Oranienburg, rendering it a complete dud. Nevertheless, Lieutenant Hopkins was hailed for his attempted sacrifice and steadfast support of his fellow airmen during a moment of crisis. His actions also seemed to ameliorate his standing with superiors, who had held him accountable for the loss of the bomb to Anderson.

ELEANOR ROOSEVELT AND Bailey Mason enjoyed a pleasant tea meeting, a monthly ritual that had solidified their friendship over the years. Bailey, wife and confidante to the enigmatic Fredrick Mason, often shared intriguing tidbits from the future during their conversations.

"So," Eleanor began, "any health advice from the future you wish to share?"

Bailey took a sip from her cup and replied, "Oh, no, not really. I do wish you had been more successful in outlawing leaded gasoline."

Eleanor sighed, "Yes, that had been a disappointment. After what you told me about that, I don't want to be anywhere near the stuff."

"As you should," Bailey agreed, "there are equal risks and all that."

"Oh, yes. That unfortunately will have to remain a long-term project, what with the southerners and all," Eleanor lamented. "Still, from what you told me, things do get better, albeit over a long period of time."

"True, we still have things in 2045 that require... errr... work."

"You know, I haven't enjoyed myself like this since Amelia disappeared," Eleanor said with a genuine smile.

"Well, thank you... I think," Bailey replied uneasily.

"Oh, you think right," Eleanor reassured her.

Suddenly, the door to the room burst open, and an exasperated aide rushed in.

"Mrs. Roosevelt," he panted, catching his breath.

"Yes, what is it?" Eleanor asked, somewhat annoyed.

"It's your husband. He's suffered a stroke."

<hr>

President Roosevelt Suffers Stroke Amidst Failed Atomic Attack on RAF Base

By Anthony Bridger
December 15 1942

In a stunning turn of events, President Franklin D. Roosevelt has suffered a stroke, dealing a significant blow to the nation's leadership at a crucial juncture in the war. This unforeseen development follows a failed attempt by German forces to launch an atomic attack on a Royal Air Force (RAF) base, marking a dark chapter in the ongoing conflict.

The ill-fated atomic bombing occurred in early December 1942 when German forces targeted an RAF base, aiming to disrupt British military operations. However, the attack met with failure, as British defenses successfully repelled the invaders, preventing catastrophic consequences that could have altered the course of the war.

The failed assault, coupled with the news of President Roosevelt's stroke, has cast a shadow over the Allied forces. The President's health has been a subject of concern, especially given his crucial role in orchestrating the war effort and maintaining the unity of the Allied nations.

Sources close to the administration report that President Roosevelt's stroke occurred shortly after receiving news of the unsuccessful atomic attack. The stress and strain of leading a nation through the global conflict undoubtedly took a toll on his health. The President is currently receiving medical attention, and the severity of the stroke remains unclear.

Vice President Henry A. Wallace assumes a pivotal role in the interim, stepping into the void left by President Roosevelt's incapacitation. Wallace's leadership will be tested as the Allies navigate through this challenging period, with critical decisions awaiting on the war front.

The failed German atomic attack underscores the escalating arms race and the desperate measures taken by the Axis powers to gain an upper hand. The world watches anxiously as these unprecedented weapons come into play, reshaping the strategies of nations embroiled in the brutal conflict.

As President Roosevelt battles the effects of his stroke, the nation must rally behind its leadership and confront the evolving challenges of the War. The failed atomic attack serves as a stark reminder of the lengths to which the Axis powers are willing to go, adding a layer of complexity to an already tumultuous period in history.

ALBERT EINSTEIN CAREFULLY set aside the papers filled with complex equations and scientific theories, joining a steadily growing pile of neglected intellectual pursuits. In recent months, the brilliant mind behind the theory of relativity had shifted his focus entirely toward a more visceral pursuit: revenge.

The cluttered workspace reflected the turmoil within Einstein's mind. Gone were the orderly stacks of scientific journals and neatly arranged research notes. Instead, a haphazard assortment of discarded calculations and unfinished equations surrounded him, a testament to his singular determination.

Einstein's hands, once accustomed to manipulating the delicate instruments of theoretical physics, now gripped a firearm with a methodical precision. Loading and aiming the gun became a ritual, a practice that demanded the same meticulous attention he had once devoted to unraveling the secrets of the universe.

As the aged physicist honed his shooting skills, a wry smile played upon his lips. There was an unexpected parallel between the pursuit of revenge and the mindset required for delving into the complexities of theoretical physics. Both endeavors demanded unwavering focus, calculated precision, and a commitment to achieving a desired outcome.

In the confines of his makeshift firing range, Einstein found solace in the routine of practicing with the firearm. Each trigger pull echoed with the determination of a man driven by a singular purpose. The act of revenge, he realized, was a primal force that could be harnessed with the same intellectual rigor he had applied to his groundbreaking scientific work.

However, Einstein acknowledged that he was not yet fully prepared. More practice, more refining of his skills, and a deeper understanding of the weapon were necessary before he could embark on the quest for retribution. In this peculiar journey, he saw the convergence of the intellectual discipline that defined his academic pursuits and the raw, instinctive energy required for an act of vengeance.

As the brilliant mind behind the theory of relativity continued his unorthodox preparations, the air in the room crackled with a peculiar energy. Albert Einstein, the renowned physicist, had become a man consumed by a different kind of equation—one that balanced the scales of justice with the weight of personal vendetta.

Chapter 11

Game of Chess

WINSTON CHURCHILL'S frustration reverberated through the war room as he slammed his fist on the desk, demanding answers in the face of the unexpected German invasion at Dover. The atmosphere was tense, with military strategists and advisors exchanging uneasy glances.

"I want answers," Churchill barked, his gaze piercing through the room. "How could we have missed this?"

The war room, usually a hub of calculated decision-making, now felt like a chamber of uncertainty. Churchill's mind raced as he considered the implications of the surprise invasion. The Germans seemed to have seized an opportunity presented by a combination of unforeseen circumstances, exploiting weaknesses in the Allied defenses.

A high-ranking military officer stepped forward, attempting to provide some clarity amidst the chaos. "Prime Minister, it appears the Germans exploited a window of vulnerability. With President Roosevelt incapacitated after the stroke, our coordination with the Americans has suffered, leaving us exposed."

Churchill sighed, acknowledging the truth in the officer's words. The absence of Roosevelt, a key ally, had disrupted the delicate balance of power and intelligence-sharing. The unpredictable nature of war had favored the Germans in this instance.

The prime minister leaned back in his chair, a heavy weariness evident in his expression. "It seems we're playing a game of chess with a bloody pigeon. What's their endgame here? This invasion seems strategically unsound."

An intelligence officer stepped forward, offering insights into the German motives. "Sir, it might be an attempt to divert our attention or force us into a hasty response. The surprise factor alone has given them an initial advantage."

Churchill nodded, his mind working to formulate a response. "Very well. We shall meet this challenge head-on. The Germans may have taken us by surprise, but they won't find victory in our weakness. Rally our forces. We'll make them regret the day they set foot on our shores."

As Churchill issued orders to fortify defenses and coordinate counterattacks, the war room transformed into a hive of strategic planning. The grim reality of war had once again tested the resilience of the Allied forces, but Churchill's determination remained unwavering. The chess match with the Germans was far from over, and Churchill was ready to outmaneuver the pigeon playing on the other side of the board.

FREDRICK MASON ENTERED the hospital room with a sense of urgency and concern etched on his face. President Franklin D. Roosevelt lay in the bed, his once formidable presence diminished by the recent stroke that had befallen him. The room was filled with an air of uncertainty, as the world outside grappled with the turmoil of World War II.

"Mr. President," Fredrick Mason greeted, his voice carrying a weight of both respect and worry. "How are you feeling?"

Roosevelt managed a weak smile. "As well as can be expected, Fred. What brings you here?"

"There's news, Mr. President. Important news," Mason replied, choosing his words carefully. He took a moment to gauge Roosevelt's condition before continuing. "The Germans have launched a full-scale invasion of Britain."

Roosevelt's eyes widened, a mix of shock and concern flickering across his face. "Britain? How could they? Have the Brits managed to hold their ground?"

Mason hesitated for a moment before delivering the next piece of information. "I'm afraid not, Mr. President. The Germans have made significant advances. London is under siege, and it seems the situation is growing dire."

Roosevelt's expression tightened, his mind grappling with the implications of the news. "This is a nightmare. We can't let Hitler take over Britain. We need to do something, Fred."

Mason nodded, his own concern mirroring Roosevelt's. "I've been working on a plan, Mr. President. Something that might give us the upper hand. But we need your approval to proceed."

Roosevelt looked at Mason, a glimmer of determination in his eyes despite his weakened state. "Tell me the plan, Fred. We can't afford to waste any time."

As Mason began outlining the details of his proposal, the hospital room transformed into a makeshift war room. The urgency of the situation pushed aside the somber atmosphere, replaced by a shared determination to confront the looming threat. In the face of adversity, these two men understood the gravity of the moment and the pivotal role they played in shaping the course of history.

BENITO MUSSOLINI'S frustration echoed through the halls of the Italian government. His supposed "allies" had left him in the dark about their plans, and now he found himself entangled in a seemingly endless war with Britain and America. Italy had been fortunate so far, spared from the brunt of heavy fighting and the devastating power of the atom bomb. Still, the mere thought of atomic warfare sent shivers down Mussolini's spine.

The lack of coordination and communication with Germany troubled Mussolini deeply. The invasion of Britain had taken him by surprise, and he resented being kept out of the loop. As the dictator of Italy, he was accustomed to being at the center of strategic decisions, not relegated to the sidelines.

Surveying the current state of affairs, Mussolini questioned whether he had chosen the right side in the war. The Americans and the British appeared to be working seamlessly together, and their collaboration seemed to yield more favorable results. Perhaps aligning more closely with the Allies could secure Italy's gains and offer a chance at a more advantageous position in the post-war landscape.

However, Mussolini recognized the need for diplomacy. Before making any drastic moves, he decided to consult with the king and the council. Such a decision would require their consent, and he couldn't risk jeopardizing the delicate balance of power within the Axis. Mussolini firmly believed in the superiority of the legacies of the Roman Empire, and he intended to navigate the complexities of global politics to ensure Italy's interests were secured.

Mussolini Offers Armistice to Allies, Pledges Support Against Germany

By Anthony Bridger,
March 20, 1943

In a shocking twist of fate, Benito Mussolini, the fascist leader of Italy, has made an unprecedented offer of an armistice to the Allied powers. The proposal, announced today, outlines Mussolini's willingness to join the war against Nazi Germany in exchange for the preservation of Italian territories gained during the conflict.

Mussolini, known for his steadfast alignment with Adolf Hitler and the Axis powers, has apparently reassessed Italy's position in the war. The sudden change in stance comes amidst growing tensions and perceived isolation within the Axis, particularly after Germany's uncoordinated invasion of Britain. It appears that Mussolini, feeling betrayed by his Axis partners, seeks a more advantageous position for Italy in the global conflict.

The offer, made through diplomatic channels, outlines Mussolini's commitment to supporting the Allied cause against Nazi Germany. In exchange, he requests the retention of territorial gains made by Italy during the war. The proposed armistice signals a significant shift in geopolitical alliances and has sparked intense discussions among Allied leaders.

Leaders of the Allied powers, including Winston Churchill and Franklin D. Roosevelt, have convened to deliberate on Mussolini's unexpected proposal. Sources close to the negotiations suggest that the Allies are cautiously considering the offer, recognizing the potential benefits of having Italy as an ally against the common enemy – Germany.

If accepted, this dramatic turn of events could reshape the dynamics of the war in Europe. Mussolini's pledge to switch sides could open up new possibilities for coordinated military actions and strategic cooperation against the Axis powers. The potential inclusion of Italian forces in the Allied war effort would undoubtedly alter the balance of power on the European front.

As the world awaits the Allies' response, the diplomatic landscape of World War II is in flux. The once unwavering bonds of the Axis powers are showing signs of strain, and Mussolini's unexpected overture may mark a pivotal moment in the global struggle for freedom and democracy.

ADOLF HITLER WAS SEETHING in rage at the moment when he was told the news. The betrayal of his "Ally" still fresh on his mind.

"The filthy Judas", he kept saying to himself, commenting on the turn of Mussolini to the allies. The man he once admired, was forever soured in his eyes.

Germany was now alone, the betrayal of Italy, Japan forced to surrender, his other allies worthless. But German air defenses remained strong, he was sure of it. His advisors hadn't told him otherwise; Germania would still win this war.

"THINGS WERE NOT GOING well for Germany", Field Marshal Erwin Rommel thought as he stood outside the Führer's bunker.

Their failed invasion of England had destroyed much of the Wehrmacht, along with tones of equipment and supplies, equipment and supplies that could have been used to defend the continent. That's not even including the mystery weapon the allies now had, one that made the atom bomb look like child's play. Now they were venerable, and an allied invasion was all but guaranteed.

All of this was not to mention revolts in the former Soviet Union, the execution of Stalin having galvanized the people there instead of putting them down. Not that he would tell the Führer any of this, nor would any of his other advisors, he did so hate bad news, even when reporting the undeniable.

The end was near, and Erwin was damn sure to guarantee he and his family were on the right side. If only he could slip his SS detail.

Germany would need a new leader after this war, as there as there was no chance Adolf Hitler and his other party members would stay in power. That he was sure of.

Chapter 12

The End is Near

"WHAT IN THE WORLD IS it with these Germans coming over to England for negotiations?" pondered Prime Minister Winston Churchill as he observed the man seated before him, guarded by a contingent of armed soldiers. The visitor seemed uneasy, constantly scanning the room as if expecting an assassin to strike at any moment – a not entirely unfounded fear given the tumultuous times.

"So," Churchill said, pouring himself a measure of brandy while eyeing his 'guest,' "what exactly leads you to believe that you can stroll in here and have your proposal accepted?" His words hung in the air, challenging the individual before him. Churchill knew the man was highly competent and qualified, even if he hailed from the opposing side – a fact that still commanded respect.

Rommel, the (now former?) Field Marshal, sat nervously, a figure Churchill had not pegged as one to betray his leader. Nevertheless, he welcomed the turn of events.

"Well," stammered Rommel, "the Führer, I mean... uh... he's losing his mind."

"I regret to inform you," replied Churchill dryly, "that he lost it a long time ago."

"Yes, ummm, well, more so than usual. And that's just from telling him the information we have shared, let alone the full picture. I expect he will do something rather... erratic when he finds out."

Churchill leaned back, taking in the gravity of the situation. "I see. So, you could read the writing on the wall and came here to avoid the consequences of your actions?"

"Well... no, not exactly," Rommel defended himself. "I did it for my family. I don't want them to face the fury of that man if I'm gone."

Churchill nodded thoughtfully. "I was told you came with some civilians. They will be safe here, that I can guarantee, as they did nothing wrong. You, on the other hand, what makes you think you wouldn't be hung alongside the rest of the Nazi leadership? After all, you didn't give that option to Stalin."

"If I am to be a dead man either way, I might as well be on the right side of history."

Churchill's eyes narrowed. "There's another reason, isn't there?"

"Well, Germany will need a new leader after the war, and occupation tends to be long... and expensive, something I assume Britain does not want to deal with."

Churchill chuckled. "That is true." His laughter echoed in the room for a moment before he became serious again. "So, you want the so-called 'throne' after the war, is that right?"

"Uh... I suppose. I mean, if there is a throne, there are still members of the royal family around."

"And I'm sure His Majesty would prefer that as well since they are his cousins. No, I was using it as a saying only."

"Of course," Rommel replied, still nervous.

Churchill continued to scrutinize the man. "I'll tell you what, I'll discuss this with the Americans to see what they think and will get back to you on that. For now, you will be taken to a prisoner-of-war camp, and a cover story will be provided to explain your presence here – though this is only for your own protection."

"I understand," Rommel said. "I take it you won't accept a handshake?"

"No, I won't. Guards?"

The two military police in the room approached Rommel, lifting him out of his chair. They soon placed him in handcuffs and escorted him out the door. Churchill, gazing out the window, couldn't believe his luck. He hoped this blow to Hitler's war machine would be the decisive factor in bringing him down for good.

FREDRICK MASON FOUND himself wrestling with insomnia when he received the news about Erwin Rommel's defection to the Allies. Despite this and Mussolini's unexpected change of allegiance, it had been a remarkably positive month for the man from the future. However, Fredrick couldn't shake the feeling that this period of bliss was too good to last. What impending events would shatter the current state of affairs?

"Can't sleep?" Bailey asked, having been inadvertently awakened by Fredrick.

"Yeah," he replied, seated at a table in the kitchen, nervously shifting in his seat.

"Why? America is winning the war, isn't it?" Bailey inquired with curiosity.

"Yeah," Fredrick agreed. "It's just a bad feeling, I guess."

"A bad feeling that is unsubstantiated, right?"

"I mean, yeah, that's true," Fredrick conceded, shrugging.

"Then don't worry about it," Bailey stated firmly.

"I know, I know. Still—"

"Still nothing," Bailey interrupted, shutting down her husband almost immediately.

Fredrick continued to gaze at his wife, somewhat unconvinced.

Bailey sighed. "You are not the president anymore; you do not have to carry the weight of the world on your shoulders. What you need to do is relax."

"Relax, in wartime?" Fredrick questioned.

"You know what I mean."

Fredrick stared at her for a few moments. "Yeah, I do."

"Good," Bailey said, running her hands on Fredrick's chest. "Now, why don't you start by going back to bed with me and counting sheep?"

"Do you mean that literally, or is it a metaphor?"

"Oh, shut up," Bailey responded, leaning in to kiss her husband on the lips. The two soon headed off to bed, seeking some well-earned rest.

EMPEROR HIROHITO GAZED somberly at the treaty laid before him, a document that symbolized Japan's defeat at the hands of the Americans. The terms were clear, and the blame for initiating the war in the Pacific would squarely fall on Japan's shoulders. Despite the bitterness of surrender, there was a glimmer of relief – the Americans had agreed to allow him to retain his throne, albeit with significantly reduced power. In the face of overwhelming defeat, Hirohito clung to the preservation of what little remained, hoping to shield Japan from further horrors.

"Please sign here," General MacArthur urged, standing behind the emperor, delivering the request in very rudimentary version of Japanese.

Emperor Hirohito took a deep breath, his hand trembling slightly as he raised the pen to sign the official instrument of surrender. In that moment, Japan surrendered its sovereignty. The negotiation for a peace agreement had been a lengthy process, but Hirohito understood that he had little choice. The war was unwinnable, and a stark reality check had been delivered by the actions of his own navy.

As the ink dried on the treaty, Emperor Hirohito could only hope that future generations would reflect on his actions with understanding. He found solace in the fact that he wasn't Tojo, his former prime minister, who now faced execution for his role in the war. The burden of history weighed heavily on Hirohito's shoulders, but he had made the choice he believed would spare Japan from further suffering.

BENITO MUSSOLINI DISEMBARKED from the plane in Dublin, a triumphant smile gracing his face. It was undeniably a very good day for Il Duce, as he prepared to meet with Churchill and Roosevelt to finalize the peace treaty that he had successfully demanded they sign in person.

The support he received from King Emmanuel and the grand council had been surprising, but it had bolstered Mussolini's confidence in his peace plan. Even the Allies, with their demand that he withdraw from Abyssinia and Egypt, were met with his eager compliance. Mussolini was more than willing to make these territorial concessions to secure the peace he desired.

However, the reaction from Hitler and the declaration of war by Germany did not catch Mussolini off guard. He had anticipated such a response and had no intention of sharing the fate that awaited the German dictator. Mussolini was keenly aware that Adolf Hitler would not live to witness the end of this war.

As Mussolini entered his waiting motorcade, the satisfaction of his gains and the successful negotiation of the treaty with the assistance of Spain and Ireland painted a confident smile on Il Duce's face. He looked forward to a new chapter with his newfound allies and hoped for a more respectful treatment in this post-war era.

PRESIDENT ROOSEVELT and Churchill patiently awaited the arrival of Il Duce for the momentous peace talks. The surprise proposal from Benito Mussolini had left Roosevelt taken aback, and the acceptance of the offer marked a significant shift, leaving Germany isolated, even with Romania and Bulgaria still in the war.

The commotion outside signaled Mussolini's arrival, and soon after, the Italian dictator entered the room. Roosevelt extended his hand in greeting, "Mr. Mussolini."

"Mister Roosevelt, Mister Churchill," Mussolini replied in somewhat broken English. "I suppose we shouldn't keep everyone waiting. Shall we proceed with this?"

The three leaders took their places at a high table, ready to address the press and finalize the peace agreement between Italy and the Allies. As they began to sign the document, formally ending hostilities, a whistling noise disrupted the proceedings.

Suddenly, a bomb crashed through the roof, plummeting into the crowded room of onlookers. Roosevelt's eyes widened in shock as he recognized the ominous object.

An explosion ensued.

FREDRICK MASON FOUND himself in a meeting with Vice President Henry Wallace, a rare occasion despite both holding significant roles in the administration. Wallace acknowledged Mason's influence on critical decisions such as the development of the atom bomb and the Laser Offensive Weaponry (LOW), as well as securing Wernher von Braun from Germany.

Vice President Wallace chuckled at the thought of the Germans having access to von Braun's expertise. "Oh yeah, that would have been a disaster. At least they had to risk their own men with the Amerikabomber; with a rocket, they wouldn't even have had to do that."

Mason nodded in agreement. "Plus, we've got a manned moon mission coming up to enjoy once the war is over."

However, their conversation was abruptly interrupted as Secret Service agents stormed into the room, urgency in their movements. The lead agent conveyed grim news to Vice President Wallace about a German air raid over Dublin and the unfortunate fate of Sphinx.

Wallace's eyes widened in shock, and he exclaimed, "No!"

The lead agent continued, "Sir, you are now the President of the United States."

Mason stood on the sidelines, grappling with disbelief as the unthinkable unfolded. All his worst fears were materializing right before him.

Chief Justice Harlan Stone entered the room, having been hastily summoned and reflecting it in his state of dress. "Mr. Vice President," he began, "I'm here to administer the oath of office."

Wallace, though shaken, took a deep breath. "I do wish my wife and kids were here, but yes."

Stone, with a solemn expression, began to administer the oath, holding out a hastily found Bible.

"I, Henry A. Wallace, do solemnly swear..."

"I, Henry A. Wallace do solemnly swear..." Wallace repeated.

"...that I will faithfully execute the Office of President of the United States....", Stone continued.

"...that I will faithfully execute the Office of President of the United States...." Wallace said.

"—and will to the best of my Ability, preserve, protect, and defend the Constitution of the United States, so help you God?"

"—and will to the best of my Ability, preserve, protect, and defend the Constitution of the United States, so help me God."

The words echoed through the room, each syllable carrying the weight of the momentous occasion. The gravity of the situation sank in for Vice President Wallace, now sworn in as the President in the face of unexpected adversity.

As Wallace took a moment to collect himself, Chief Justice Stone nodded in acknowledgment. "Mr. President," he said plainly, offering a reassuring pat on Wallace's shoulder.

The Secret Service agents exchanged concerned glances, aware of the challenges that lay ahead. Mason, still grappling with the sudden turn of events, approached the new President.

"Sir, we need to assess the situation and discuss our response strategy," Mason suggested, recognizing the urgency of the matter.

President Wallace, regaining his composure, nodded. "Right. Let's convene an emergency meeting. We need to address this crisis and make decisions that will shape the course of our response."

The group hastily moved to a secure conference room, leaving President Wallace alone with Mr. Mason once more.

"I feel as if the weight of the world has been just dropped on me", President Wallace said.

"It has", Mr. Mason said, laying a hand on the man's shoulder. "I do hope that I'm not being imprudent in that I do have a recommendation for a vice president in the 1944 election."

"Is it you?" Wallace questioned.

"No", Mr. Mason replied. "Do you remember a senator by the name of Harry Truman?"

Chapter 13

Escalations

Tragedy Strikes in Dublin: FDR Falls Victim to Bombing During Peace Conference

April 16, 1943

By Anthony Bridger

Yesterday, in a shocking turn of events, a bombing orchestrated by Nazi Germany has claimed the life of President Franklin D. Roosevelt, casting a dark shadow over the peace talks in Dublin. The conference, aimed at establishing peace between the Allies and Italy, took an unforeseen and tragic turn, altering the course of history.

President Roosevelt, who had been instrumental in the war effort, was attending the conference alongside prominent leaders, including Winston Churchill and Benito Mussolini. The historic gathering aimed to negotiate a peace agreement that could reshape the geopolitical landscape. However, the conference turned into a scene of chaos and destruction.

The Nazi bombing targeted the venue of the peace talks, resulting in the loss of many lives, including that of the esteemed President Roosevelt. The shockwaves from this tragic incident reverberated through the international community, leaving leaders and citizens alike in mourning.

With Roosevelt's untimely death, Vice President Henry Wallace is thrust into the presidency during this critical juncture in history. Wallace, previously serving as Vice President, now faces the daunting task of leading the nation through the ongoing war and continuing the pursuit of peace.

Meanwhile, amidst the devastation, both Winston Churchill and Benito Mussolini have survived the attack. Their fate, now intertwined with the uncertain future of global politics, adds further complexity to an already tumultuous time.

Ireland, the host of the ill-fated peace conference, has declared war on Nazi Germany in response to the bombing. The Irish government, expressing outrage at the indiscriminate act of violence on their soil, has taken a bold step into the conflict, aligning themselves against the Axis powers.

As the world grapples with the repercussions of this tragic event, the loss of President Roosevelt marks a somber moment in history. The path to peace remains uncertain, and the global community must now navigate the challenges that lie ahead without the steady guidance of the leader who played a pivotal role in shaping the Allied forces.

A MONTH HAD PASSED since the tragic events in Dublin, and President Henry Wallace found himself still grappling with the weight of unexpected responsibilities. Despite the inner turmoil, he maintained a stoic exterior, understanding that strength was required in this moment of crisis. Little did the nation know, Wallace had not only been thrust into the presidency but had also discovered the extraordinary truth about his special advisor, Fredrick Mason—a man from the future.

The revelation of Mr. Mason's origin had been a profound shock, yet Wallace saw no reason to doubt the advisor, especially considering Roosevelt's trust in him. Nevertheless, as the war raged on and the nation faced uncertainties, Wallace understood the imperative of leading with unwavering resolve.

The burdens on Wallace's shoulders seemed insurmountable—an unexpected presidency, a war to prosecute, and the looming specter of an upcoming election. It was a delicate balancing act, one that required him to navigate the complexities of wartime strategy while keeping an eye on the political horizon.

Both Winston Churchill and Benito Mussolini, key allies in this global conflict, had recovered substantially from their injuries but found themselves ironically confined to wheelchairs. With their incapacitation for the past month, the weight of strategic decisions rested largely on Wallace's shoulders. The president found himself in a pivotal meeting with General Dwight D. Eisenhower, catching up on critical plans for the impending invasion of mainland Europe.

"We believe a large, overwhelming landing force split into five groups at Normandy would be the best option to establish both a beachhead and foothold on mainland Europe," General Eisenhower stated with an air of strategic authority, laying out the ambitious plan before President Wallace.

Eisenhower's proposal outlined a coordinated effort that, when combined with existing forces in the Mediterranean, aimed to encircle German forces in France and set the stage for a rapid liberation of the region. The ultimate goal was to either push into Germany proper or force a surrender from the Axis powers.

As Wallace contemplated the gravity of the plan, he absentmindedly stroked his unshaven chin, a testament to the mounting stress he bore. Seeking insight, he turned to his trusted advisor, Fredrick Mason, the only other person present in the room besides Eisenhower.

"Sir," Eisenhower interjected, somewhat skeptical, "are you sure you want to consult with a civilian for this?"

"Franklin Roosevelt trusted Mr. Mason, and I do as well," Wallace replied calmly, emphasizing his confidence in Mr. Mason's judgment.

Mr. Mason, in turn, weighed in on the military strategy. "As it is, I agree with this plan. Despite the inherent danger, it seems to be the only viable option since both atomic and LOW weaponry have failed to subdue Germany thus far."

With consensus reached among the trio, President Wallace nodded and closed his eyes momentarily, taking a deep breath. "Okay, let's do it."

"Yes, sir," Eisenhower acknowledged, ready to set the wheels in motion. He efficiently gathered up his plans and other classified documents, preparing to execute the mission.

"Notify who you need, but let's keep this tight-lipped, shall we?" Wallace directed, emphasizing the need for secrecy.

"Understood, sir," Eisenhower replied with a salute before exiting the Oval Office.

Alone with Mr. Mason, President Wallace slumped back in his chair, wearied by the weight of leadership. "You said you were president in your time."

"Yes," Mr. Mason confirmed.

"Tell me, does this job ever get easier?" Wallace inquired, seeking a glimpse into the challenges that lay ahead.

"Afraid not," Mr. Mason responded. "The United States becomes a superpower after the war, and with the Soviet Union now gone, probably the sole one at that."

Wallace grumbled, realizing the complexities awaiting him. "Perfect, just perfect." The burden of leadership, it seemed, was a timeless challenge.

ALBERT EINSTEIN WAS profoundly disturbed by the news of Franklin Roosevelt's assassination at the hands of the Germans. In the midst of an ongoing war, the unexpected nature of Roosevelt's murder seemed particularly heinous, a calculated move by Hitler that added another layer to the dictator's list of crimes.

The former academic, now fueled by a thirst for revenge, meticulously cleaned his gun, the cold metal a symbol of the impending retribution he sought. Practicing the routine of loading and unloading the weapon had become a ritual for Einstein over the past several months. Each click and slide of the mechanism echoed his determination to bring justice for the fallen president.

As he honed his skills with the firearm, Einstein pondered the aftermath of his quest for retribution. The jail cell that awaited him if he succeeded was a mere inconvenience, for he believed he could continue his intellectual pursuits even within the confines of imprisonment. While his reputation might be tarnished, the pursuit of justice took precedence.

The eminent physicist knew that the path he was embarking upon would lead to consequences beyond personal sacrifice. Yet, driven by a sense of moral duty and the desire to avenge Roosevelt, Einstein steeled himself for the inevitable confrontation with the tyrannical forces that had disrupted the course of history.

ADOLF HITLER SEETHED in a storm of frustration, pondering the twists of fate that had led to the unraveling of his once seemingly invincible empire. The atom bomb, long-range bombers, and dominance over Europe were all assets he possessed, yet everything was slipping through his fingers. The sudden and overwhelming turn of events bewildered him, and the sense of impending defeat gnawed at his very core.

While the successful elimination of Roosevelt, the crippling of Churchill, and the betrayal of Mussolini had provided some solace, it was not enough to stem the relentless advance of the Allies. Hitler, who considered his genius the linchpin holding Germany together, found himself grappling with the inexplicable unraveling of his grand vision.

Amidst his internal turmoil, a subordinate hastily entered the bunker, interrupting Hitler's brooding thoughts. The young aide, standing at attention, delivered an urgent message from France, prompting Hitler's half-hearted interest.

"What is it?" the Führer inquired, his attention divided.

"This morning, the Allies launched their invasion of France," the aide reported, presenting the critical information.

Hitler, perhaps hoping for a predictable scenario, questioned, "At Calais, as expected?"

The aide hesitated before delivering the unexpected blow. "Mein Führer, the Allies have landed at Normandy."

Hitler, momentarily bereft of words, removed his glasses and sank into his chair. Dismissing the aide with a wave, he descended into a renewed fit of ranting and raving, grappling with the realization that his once unassailable fortress was now under siege from an unforeseen quarter.

REGARDLESS OF HIS DOCTOR'S admonitions, Winston Churchill remained resolute in his habits, indulging in brandy and cigars. Today, particularly, seemed fitting for such vices, as it marked a time of celebration—the commencement of the liberation of Europe at the beaches of Normandy.

While it wasn't the envisioned scenario of Britain single-handedly rescuing Europe, with the Americans, Canadians, and even the Irish contributing, a victory was a victory. The rapid progress exceeded expectations, and Churchill found himself adjusting to the leadership of Henry Wallace, who, so far, had proven himself worthy. However, the indelible mark left by Franklin Roosevelt still loomed large, casting a shadow over the proceedings.

THE TWO PRESIDENTS

Pouring another drink, Churchill reflected on the favorable reports streaming in, detailing the advancements made on the Normandy beaches. A successful beachhead had been established, signaling a promising turn of events.

Raising his glass, Churchill offered a solitary toast, "To events to come, and victory." Though uttered in an empty room, he considered his words a proclamation of wisdom. Downing the beverage, a satisfied smile graced his face. In Churchill's view, good things were on the horizon, a certainty that fueled his optimism in the face of unfolding events.

"THE PEOPLE OF UKRAINE have endured enough," resonated the collective sentiments of millions of Ukrainians. Their history had been marred by oppression under Russian rule, and the recent German occupation had only exacerbated their plight. However, today marked a turning point—today, they would seize their freedom.

The successful Allied invasion of France, though initially subdued in its reach, had ignited a spark of hope within the Slavic nation. The yearning for freedom, suppressed for far too long, now surged through the hearts of the Ukrainian people. Their determination to break free from the shackles of occupation overshadowed any fear of the costs involved.

Remarkably, the rebellion organized itself with a speed that defied expectations. Partisans swiftly took control of major cities across Ukraine within a week, even as German and Romanian forces maintained a grip on substantial portions of the country. The Ukrainian partisans, fueled by an unwavering resolve, mirrored the resilience of the Yugoslav partisans who had preceded them.

As the liberation efforts gained momentum, Ukraine envisioned a future liberated from both Russian and German oppression. In a strategic move, the Ukrainian and Yugoslav partisans joined forces, embarking on a collaborative journey to liberate the Balkans. Together, they forged a path towards independence, united by a shared commitment to freeing their lands from the yoke of tyranny.

Chapter 14

Collapse

Allied Forces Launch Successful Invasion on Occupied France
By Anthony Bridger,
August 16, 1943

In an audacious move that has already altered the course of the war, Allied forces orchestrated a triumphant invasion of France, liberating the shores of Normandy and marking a decisive turn in the European conflict.

The surprise invasion, originally anticipated not to take place until 1944, took place on the morning of August 15th, catching Axis forces off guard. Led by General Dwight D. Eisenhower, the Allies landed troops from the United States, United Kingdom, Canada, Ireland, and other nations, establishing a crucial beachhead and setting the stage for the liberation of occupied Europe.

Reports from the front lines indicate that the operation has been a resounding success, with Allied forces securing key positions and pushing inland against German defenses. The liberated cities of Normandy now echo with the cheers of both soldiers and grateful civilians.

Simultaneously, reports have come in that the people of Ukraine have risen against their oppressors, fueled by news of the successful Allied invasion. Tired of enduring both Russian and German occupation, millions of Ukrainians have rallied in a coordinated uprising, seizing control of major cities within a week.

Partisan forces, mirroring the successes of their Yugoslav counterparts, have rapidly organized and begun the liberation of Ukraine. This unexpected surge in resistance is not only a testament to the indomitable spirit of the Ukrainian people but also a strategic blow to the remaining Axis powers.

As the world watches the events unfolding on the Western Front and in the streets of Ukrainian cities, the Allies are on the brink of reshaping the future of Europe and bringing an end to the tyranny that has plagued the continent for far too long.

The coming days will undoubtedly see further developments, but for now, the Allied forces celebrate a significant step towards the liberation of Europe.

BERLIN, THE ONCE-MAJESTIC capital of Germany and the Third Reich, now finds itself ensconced in the tightening grip of

Allied forces. The swift and unexpected collapse of the once-invincible German war machine, achieved in under seven months, has sent shockwaves through the demoralized population. Plans that were originally drawn up to confront prolonged resistance for years are now rendered obsolete, leaving only the staunchest of believers to wage a last stand.

The elusive Adolf Hitler, conspicuous in his absence, is said to be concealed somewhere within the labyrinthine depths of Berlin, perhaps holed up in an underground bunker. The Allies, determined to hold him accountable for heinous crimes against humanity, have issued a categorical order: capture Hitler alive, if possible.

The cityscape, once a testament to Germany's power and grandeur, now lies in ruins. The deployment of the Allies' enigmatic and devastating LOW weaponry has reduced Berlin to rubble, leaving survivors bewildered and seeking answers. The origin and capabilities of this mysterious weapon remain a closely guarded secret, with the Americans revealing little about their newfound and formidable power.

The skies above Berlin echo with the ominous sounds of destruction as LOW-equipped aircraft systematically target strategic locations. Despite the devastation, resilient survivors emerge from the debris, confronting a city forever changed by the relentless onslaught.

As the net tightens around Berlin, rumors circulate about the mental state of Adolf Hitler, with reports suggesting that the once-fearful dictator may be on the verge of cracking. Special advisor Fredrick Mason, armed with information that could expedite the Allies' victory, maintains a steely resolve to uncover

Hitler's elusive hiding place. The good news was, he knew exactly where to find the elusive dictator.

Throughout the city, the remnants of die-hard believers, the last holdouts of the Nazi ideology, continue to resist the advancing Allied forces. In the face of certain defeat, these fervent loyalists cling to their convictions, refusing to acknowledge the looming downfall of the Third Reich.

Amidst the ruins, the world watches with anticipation as the Allies encircle Berlin. The end of Hitler's tyrannical regime appears to be within reach, and the once-mighty Third Reich teeters on the brink of collapse.

ADOLF HITLER PACED frantically within the confined space of his bunker, gripping a gun in one hand and clutching cyanide pills in the other. The imminent collapse of his regime left him with no intention of facing capture; he was determined to evade the justice that awaited him. Even his loyal companion, Blondie the dog, had met a grim end, and now his wife Eva Braun stood by, ready to join him in death.

The bewildered dictator struggled to comprehend the sudden unraveling of his grand design. Victory had seemed assured, and he basked in the belief of German superiority. Yet, an unseen force, a mysterious and devastating weapon wielded by the Allies, had shattered his illusions, bringing about a precipitous downfall.

In the midst of his contemplations, a deafening bang reverberated through the bunker, jolting Hitler from his thoughts. Chaos ensued with shouts and gunfire signaling the arrival of the Allies to the bunker. The moment had arrived; his final stand was at hand.

Turning to Eva with a solemn expression, Hitler uttered, "My love, it is time."

Eva, her eyes brimming with tears, nodded in agreement, clasping her own cyanide capsules. Summoning a brave façade, she placed the capsules in her mouth, mirroring her husband's actions.

Before the fateful bite, however, an abrupt intrusion disrupted their macabre pact. Allied soldiers descended upon them, forcefully prying open their mouths and preventing the tragic consummation.

Hitler tried to pullout his pistol that he held and use that instead, but found another arm grabbing him, and prying it out of his fingers. The once feared doctor was now helpless, and a prisoner of the allied powers. The war, was all but over.

***

Hitler Captured: The Beginning of the End for Axis Forces

By Anthony Bridger
March 10, 1944

In a stunning turn of events that signals a turning point in the ongoing global conflict, Adolf Hitler, the notorious leader of the Axis forces, has been captured by American troops. This development marks a critical juncture in the war and is likely to hasten the crumbling of Axis resistance across Europe.

Reports confirm that American forces successfully apprehended Hitler in an undisclosed location, dealing a significant blow to the already demoralized German forces. Hitler, who once reveled in the illusion of invincibility, now finds himself at the mercy of the Allies.

The capture comes on the heels of relentless Allied offensives, coupled with the deployment of mysterious and powerful weapons that have left the Axis forces reeling. The fall of Berlin, surrounded by the devastation wrought by innovative weaponry, set the stage for the ultimate capture of the Führer.

General Dwight D. Eisenhower, leading the charge against Axis strongholds, expressed optimism about the recent developments. "This is a monumental achievement for the Allied forces. Hitler's capture sends a clear message to the remaining Axis troops that their leader has been brought to justice, and it's time for them to lay down their arms."

The news of Hitler's capture has ignited a wave of surrender among Axis holdouts. With the linchpin of their ideology now in custody, loyalists are left with dwindling morale and a stark realization that the war's tide has irrevocably shifted against them.

The aftermath of Hitler's capture is expected to unravel the remnants of the once-mighty Axis powers. As the world anxiously awaits further details on the fate of the fallen dictator, it is undeniable that the end of this global conflict is within sight, and a new era of peace may soon emerge from the shadows of war-torn Europe.

MR. MASON EXHALED A sigh of relief, his shoulders visibly relaxing as the weight of war seemed to lift from them. The war was finally over, and he found himself in London, representing President Wallace. The new president had leaned heavily on Mr. Mason during the transitional period, a responsibility that both honored and worried him.

"Well, that's life," he mused, accepting the reality of his role. His eyes scanned the horizon, waiting for the arrival of his VIP.

"Say, am I too late, chap?" inquired a familiar British voice. Turning to his right, Mr. Mason was greeted by Winston Churchill, who was no longer confined to a wheelchair.

"No, I would say you are just in time," Mr. Mason replied, acknowledging Churchill's presence with a nod.

"Good," Churchill declared with a determined glint in his eyes. "I have been looking forward to seeing this."

A shout from the crowd drew their attention. Following the gaze, they saw a propeller plane with distinctive U.S. Army markings approaching one of Heathrow's runways. The aircraft gracefully descended, landing with precision as armed personnel secured the area.

"There it is," someone exclaimed, capturing the collective sentiment. The door to the plane swung open, revealing the captive figures of Adolf Hitler, bound in chains, and his wife Eva Braun. A satisfying smile played on Mr. Mason's lips – the orchestrator of immense suffering was not escaping justice this time.

To Mr. Mason's surprise, Joseph Goebbels was also in chains, following closely behind Hitler and Eva Braun. The successful capture of the entire bunker's occupants was a notable achievement, especially when compared to his original timeline. Reports indicated that this time, much of the Nazi high command was either captured or confirmed dead, with the only exception being the elusive Adolf Eichmann.

Mr. Mason couldn't help but shrug. "You can't win them all," he thought, foreseeing future challenges for Israel in the 1960s. He made a mental note to share this information with President Wallace.

The trio of captives was efficiently loaded into a military vehicle, surrounded by vigilant armed guards. Departing swiftly, the vehicle headed for a more secure and undisclosed location.

Turning back to Churchill, Mr. Mason noticed the widest smile on the former Prime Minister's face. "You don't know how long I have been waiting to see that," Churchill declared.

"I think I have an idea," Mr. Mason responded with a knowing nod.

"Well, I believe that concludes our business for today then," Churchill remarked, extending his hand for a handshake.

Accepting the handshake, Mr. Mason seized the opportunity for a question. "As you know, America prides itself on democracy and elections. Will Britain be doing the same soon, now that the war is over?"

"Oh, yes," Churchill replied. "Although it won't be with me at the helm."

"Really?" Mr. Mason raised an eyebrow at this revelation. It contradicted his recollection of events.

"Yes, well, I am confident in my party's chances. However, I suffered a grave injury and had the weight of the world on my shoulders. It would be good to get some time off," Churchill explained.

Mr. Mason smiled. "Good luck wherever you go, then." Privately, he knew for a fact that the Tories were destined to lose the next election, but he wisely kept that thought to himself.

With that, Churchill departed, leaving Mr. Mason alone once again. There was a lot of work to do, and several countries to rebuild. This responsibility fell to America and Britain, what with the collapse of the Soviet Union. He wondered what other changes this would bring. He took a deep breath, that was a problem for another day.

Chapter 15

Punishment

"ALL RISE FOR THE HONORABLE judges," echoed the authoritative call of a military officer, functioning as the bailiff. With a swift response, everyone in the makeshift courtroom stood as a panel of judges entered, taking their respective seats, setting the stage for the trial that was about to unfold.

"Adolf Hitler, please stand," instructed the lead judge. A disheveled, mustached man obeyed the command. To Fredrick Mason, it was a surreal sight; a year ago, identifying this man as Adolf Hitler would have seemed unfathomable.

"You stand here accused of war crimes, crimes against peace, and crimes against humanity. A trial was subsequently held, and this panel unanimously has gone on to find you guilty of all charges," declared the lead prosecutor. A wave of cheering rippled through the assembled listeners, but the lead judge swiftly hushed the crowd.

"Thus, it falls on this council to pass its decision on your punishment for your crimes." The courtroom buzzed with anticipation as the crowd leaned in to catch the pronouncement.

"After careful consideration and unanimous agreement, this council has decided to exile you for life to the farthest point on earth possible from Berlin, to the British territory of the Picairian Islands in the South Pacific." The lead judge brought down the gavel, finalizing their decision.

The room exploded into pandemonium, a cacophony of disbelief and outrage echoing through the space. The decision to give Adolf Hitler the 'Napoleon treatment,' allowing him to live out his days in exile, sparked intense debate about the nature of justice. Many questioned the appropriateness of such leniency, given the gravity of Hitler's crimes.

For Hitler himself, his demeanor appeared to be a puzzle, a complex mix of emotions simmering beneath a seemingly calm exterior. Mr. Mason found it disconcerting, unable to decipher the thoughts swirling within the man's mind. This uncertainty unsettled him.

The lenient treatment Hitler received stood in stark contrast to the harsh sentences handed down to other party officials, many of whom faced death or hard labor. Mr. Mason couldn't fathom how Hitler secured such a comparatively mild punishment. Was there still an undercurrent of sympathy for him among the judges? The resurgence of fascism in the U.S. and Britain before the war, and its lingering issues in 2045, nagged at Mr. Mason's concerns.

Sighing in resignation, the man from the future recognized the limitations of his influence. The decision of the assembled judges was final, and he could do nothing to alter it. The will of the court had spoken, and Hitler's fate was sealed.

Without uttering another word, the former Führer of Germany, Adolf Hitler, was hoisted out of his chair and forcibly escorted towards the courtroom exit. A swarm of journalists trailed behind, hungry for any glimpse of the disgraced dictator.

Meanwhile, Mr. Mason chose to remain behind. As the room emptied, only he and the lead judge, Mr. Stewart, were left.

"Mr. Stewart," Mr. Mason called out to the stern judge, who turned to face him.

"Yes, Mr. Mason," responded the stalwart man.

"In my report to the president, I would like to understand why you have opted for such a... Napoleonic-style punishment for a man who sought to conquer Europe and perpetrate genocide against the Jews," inquired Mr. Mason.

Mr. Stewart scoffed dismissively, eliciting a raised eyebrow from Mr. Mason.

"Why should I care about what a pretender to the presidency wants? Or how those rat bastards were treated?" retorted Mr. Stewart with disdain.

Mr. Mason's eyes widened at the judge's callous response. "Careful there, Stewart, you're treading dangerous waters."

Again, Mr. Stewart scoffed. "I don't know why you care about them so much. The previous pretender evacuated a large chunk of them to Alaska!" he spat out the words with vehement hatred.

"Where they were annihilated by a nuclear weapon on Hitler's orders, despite New Jerusalem not being a military target or of strategic importance!" Mr. Mason countered passionately.

"Bah," Mr. Stewart scoffed again. "What they did to the world? They deserved it. Honestly, the Führer should have done more!"

As if unable to contain himself, Mr. Stewart seemed on the verge of saying more but was abruptly halted by a punch to the mouth, courtesy of Mr. Mason.

"Ahhh! What the hell, Mason?" cried out Mr. Stewart, nursing his injured mouth.

"I'll be sure to let the president know what you said about 'those people' and the 'previous guy.' He will definitely find it interesting," Mr. Mason delivered this declaration with a coldness he didn't know he possessed. He then turned around and left the room, leaving Mr. Stewart alone on the floor, with a bloody nose.

Stepping outside, Mr. Mason found himself amidst a scene of utter chaos. Perplexed, he pondered, "What was going on? What had he missed?" The atmosphere was charged with tension as military police darted about, detaining a white-haired man who, upon closer inspection, appeared to be none other than Albert Einstein. A renowned physicist in handcuffs — a sight that left Mr. Mason bewildered. "What was Einstein doing here?" he wondered.

His curiosity piqued, Mr. Mason continued scanning the tumultuous scene. Not far away, a group of military police huddled around a figure on the ground. As he approached, ready to inquire about the unfolding situation, he abruptly halted. His eyes widened with recognition — the lifeless body was Adolf Hitler.

The German dictator bore a gunshot wound, the red stain of fresh blood still visible. Lifeless eyes stared blankly at the sky. It was at this moment that Mr. Mason began connecting the dots. Albert Einstein had, it seemed, assassinated Adolf Hitler. The gravity of the situation hung in the air, and Mr. Mason grappled with the enormity of the event that had just unfolded before him.

Mr. Mason stood there, absorbing the surreal scene. The juxtaposition of Einstein in custody and Hitler's lifeless body on the ground was an inconceivable tableau. He couldn't fathom the implications of what he was witnessing. What had transpired to lead to this shocking turn of events?

As military police continued their hurried activities, Mr. Mason couldn't help but wonder about the motivations behind

Einstein's drastic actions. Was it a personal vendetta, an act of revenge, or perhaps a desperate attempt to prevent further atrocities? The questions swirled in his mind as he grappled with the unexpected twists in this already tumultuous chapter of history.

The gravity of the situation began to sink in. Hitler, once a symbol of tyrannical power, now lay lifeless on the ground, his reign of terror seemingly ended by the hand of a scientist. Mr. Mason contemplated the potential repercussions of this extraordinary event, recognizing that the world would be forever changed by the demise of the man who had orchestrated one of the darkest periods in history.

He pondered the reactions that would undoubtedly ripple through the global community and the impact this dramatic turn would have on the ongoing legal proceedings. The trial had just concluded, and now a new chapter unfolded with a stunning twist that no one could have foreseen. The man from the future found himself at the center of a historical juncture, navigating the uncertain aftermath of an assassination that held the potential to reshape the course of postwar justice.

***

Einstein's Shocking Act: Assassination in Nuremberg Alters Postwar Narrative

By Anthony Bridger
May 17, 1944

In an unforeseen turn of events following the trial and exile of Adolf Hitler, the city of Nuremberg in Germany became the stage for an extraordinary act that has sent shockwaves through the world. Albert Einstein, the renowned physicist, long known for his brilliance and pacifist stance, emerged from two years of reclusion to deliver his own form of justice.

Einstein's self-imposed exile, prompted by the horrific events of the nuclear bombing of New Jerusalem, Alaska, had transformed him into a recluse, withdrawn from the scientific and political circles he once graced. However, recent events seem to have shaken him from his solitude.

As Hitler, the mastermind behind one of history's darkest periods, was to be exiled to the remote British territory of the Pitcairn islands, the world anticipated a seemingly fitting but lenient punishment. Little did anyone expect that Einstein, fueled by an amalgamation of personal grief and a desire to end further atrocities, would take matters into his own hands.

The city of Nuremberg, a symbolic location for Nazi rallies during the regime, suddenly became a backdrop for an act of vigilantism that defied the norms of postwar justice. Witnesses recount a chaotic scene as military police apprehended Einstein immediately after the assassination. The once-revered scientist, now in custody, seemed to have traded his pursuit of knowledge for an unthinkable act of retribution.

The circumstances surrounding Einstein's actions remain shrouded in mystery. What led the brilliant mind to such drastic measures? Was it a response to the suffering inflicted upon his people, a retaliation for the devastation of New Jerusalem, or an effort to prevent Hitler from escaping justice in exile?

The international community now grapples with the aftermath of this astonishing event. Hitler, who had faced exile as his penance, instead met a violent end at the hands of a figure renowned for intellectual pursuits rather than acts of aggression.

As the world watches, awaiting further developments and official statements, Nuremberg stands as a symbol of unexpected upheaval. The legacy of Einstein's actions will undoubtedly linger, forcing humanity to confront the complex interplay of justice, morality, and the consequences of wartime atrocities.

PRESIDENT WALLACE SLAMMED the newspaper onto the resolute desk, his frustration palpable. He needed answers, an explanation for the unexpected turn of events that saw the renowned physicist, Albert Einstein, assassinate Adolf Hitler immediately following his trial and unexpected exile.

"How can something like this happen?" President Wallace exclaimed with a mix of anger and disbelief.

"I don't know; nothing like this happened in the original timeline," Mr. Mason responded, defending himself. "Hitler took his own life there, with lingering conspiracies suggesting he fled to Argentina."

President Wallace grasped the bridge of his nose, clearly weighed down by the gravity of the situation. "I almost wish that's how things played out here," he admitted, sighing as he sank back into his chair, exhausted.

"Mr. President?" Mr. Mason called out, concerned for a man thrust into a role he was never supposed to assume.

"Look, I know you're trying to create a better timeline than the one you had, but is all of this really worth it?" President Wallace questioned, expressing the doubt that lingered in the air.

Fredrick took a moment to ponder the question before responding, "I don't know if this was worth it or not."

"What?" President Wallace asked, visibly surprised by the honesty of the answer.

"I don't know if it was worth it or not," Mr. Mason reiterated. "Sure, more lives were saved among the troops, but at the cost of higher civilian casualties and the tarnishing of a great mind's reputation."

"But it's Hitler he shot," President Wallace remarked dismissively.

"True, but that's not the point," Mr. Mason replied, maintaining his composure. "I simply don't know, and I admit that."

President Wallace stared at the man from the future for a moment before quietly saying, "I agree."

"What?" Mr. Mason asked, now the one taken aback.

"I agree with your statement, and I admire a man who can admit when he doesn't know."

"Thank you, sir," Mr. Mason responded, still bewildered.

President Wallace leaned back in his chair, tenting his hands together. "I've been thinking about what you told me, to pick Harry Truman as my running mate in the upcoming election."

"Yes?" Mr. Mason inquired.

"I'm not sure that's a good idea."

"What?" Mr. Mason said, surprised. "Why not?"

"You said he became president in your timeline after the death of Franklin Roosevelt. Here, I became president instead. I'm sure the conservatives in the party would be happy to make him my Vice President, but I believe there's someone better qualified for the times we now find ourselves in.

"Who?" Mr. Mason asked, though deep down, he already knew the answer.

"You," President Wallace declared.

Chapter 16

A New World Order

IT MARKED THE GRANDEST congregation of diplomats ever assembled—the birth of the United Nations. A beacon of hope emerged, signaling an era where disputes could be settled through dialogue rather than devastating warfare. At least, that was Mr. Mason's hopeful vision for the United Nations this time.

"All rise for the Honorable Fredrick Mason of the United States of America, without whom this assembly wouldn't be possible," the sergeant at arms proclaimed. Applause thundered through the hall as Mr. Mason ascended to the podium. He patiently waited for the fervor to subside before commencing his opening speech, an address meant to officially inaugurate the United Nations.

Taking in the array of distinguished diplomats and world leaders from various nations, Mr. Mason felt a profound sense of responsibility. The birth of the United Nations was a culmination of efforts to prevent the horrors of war from plaguing humanity again. He cleared his throat and began his speech.

"Ladies and gentlemen, esteemed delegates, and honored guests, I stand before you today with a profound sense of purpose and gratitude. The establishment of the United Nations marks a pivotal moment in history – a moment where nations come together not just to secure peace, but to forge a future of cooperation, understanding, and shared prosperity.

As we look back on the devastation caused by conflicts that have marred our world, we recognize the need for a new era, one in which diplomacy triumphs over hostility and understanding prevails over ignorance. The United Nations, born out of the collective desire for a better world, represents our commitment to this noble cause.

Today, as we embark on this journey of collaboration, let us reflect on the sacrifices made, the lessons learned, and the common ground that unites us all. The challenges ahead are many, but together, united, we can overcome them. The ideals that bind us are not just words on paper; they are the shared aspirations of humanity.

We stand at the crossroads of history, and the choices we make will define the legacy we leave for future generations. It is our duty to foster dialogue, seek common ground, and strive for a world where conflicts are resolved through peaceful means.

The United Nations is not just an organization; it is a beacon of hope, a testament to our collective commitment to creating a world where justice, equality, and human rights are upheld. Let us work together, hand in hand, to build a future where the bonds of peace are stronger than the shackles of war.

May this assembly serve as a reminder that our differences are opportunities for understanding, and our unity is the key to a brighter tomorrow. As we officially open the United Nations, let us embark on a journey of cooperation, compassion, and progress.

Thank you, and may this endeavor be a testament to the resilience of the human spirit and the possibilities that arise when nations come together in pursuit of a better world."

The applause was resounding. The United Nations was officially open for business. Fredrick Mason couldn't be happier.

Wallace and Mason Triumph in Historic 1944 Presidential Election

By Anthony Bridger
November 10, 1944

In a stunning turn of events, President Henry Wallace and his unconventional but influential advisor, Fredrick Mason, secured a resounding victory in the 1944 presidential election. The election, held in the wake of the end of World War II and amid global efforts for reconstruction, witnessed a groundbreaking victory for the Democratic duo.

President Wallace, who assumed office following the tragic death of Franklin D. Roosevelt, led the nation through the final stages of the war, steering the United States towards a pivotal role in shaping the post-war world. The unexpected decision to bring Mason on as his running mate raised eyebrows, but it appears to have resonated with a significant portion of the American electorate.

The duo's victory sends a clear message that the American public values a vision for a new world order, built on diplomacy, collaboration, and the principles of the recently established United Nations. Wallace and Mason's platform emphasized a commitment to international cooperation, ensuring that the United States would play a leading role in fostering global unity and rebuilding war-torn nations.

Mason's influence, stemming from his unique insights into the future, seemed to have resonated with voters who sought a departure from traditional political norms. The nation, hungry for stability and progress after the devastation of war, found solace in the promises of a forward-thinking administration.

As the results poured in, it became evident that the Wallace-Mason ticket had secured not only the support of Democrats but also garnered substantial bipartisan backing. The election outcome reflects a collective desire for a fresh approach to governance, marked by visionary leadership and a commitment to shaping a better world.

The victory ceremony held in Washington D.C. saw President Wallace and Vice President Mason expressing their gratitude to the American people. Wallace pledged to lead the nation into an era of peace, economic recovery, and international cooperation. Mason, known for his unorthodox yet effective contributions, vowed to support the president in implementing their shared vision.

FOR THE FIRST TIME in what felt like an eternity, Fredrick Mason found himself in a state of relaxation. The weight of war, the intricacies of navigating a new timeline, and the responsibilities of his role had taken their toll over the years. Now, with a moment to breathe, he savored the tranquility alongside his wife, Bailey.

Bailey wrapped her arms around Fredrick, a warm embrace that spoke volumes about the solace they found in each other's company. "You seem genuinely relaxed," she observed.

Fredrick chuckled. "Can you blame me? It's been non-stop for so long. Now, with the vice presidency thrown into the mix, I guess I'm due for a break."

Bailey playfully kissed Fredrick on the cheek, her affectionate gesture prompting a blush. "How did you end up as Vice President anyway?" she inquired.

"I wish I had a straightforward answer for that, but it just happened," Fredrick admitted with a shrug.

Bailey grinned. "Well, whatever the reason, you've earned this downtime."

As the couple settled into the comfort of their home, Bailey pondered their options for the day. "Any specific plans or desires?"

Fredrick thought for a moment. "With rationing still in place and many places closed, options are a bit limited."

"Who needs fancy outings anyway?" Bailey teased. "A cozy day at home can be just as delightful."

"I couldn't agree more," Fredrick replied.

"Then let us just enjoy each other's company," Bailey suggested with a smile. Fredrick reciprocated the smile, grateful for the simple pleasures and the extraordinary woman beside him. While part of him occasionally yearned for a return to 2045, he was determined to embrace the present and make the most of every moment.

FOR PRESIDENT WALLACE, the recent reports were deeply unsettling. The relationship between the United States and Britain, forged in the crucible of World War II, was now showing signs of strain. Fredrick Mason's earlier warnings about a potential Cold War, initially dismissed given the collapse of the Soviet Union, now seemed to be materializing in a different form.

The catalyst for this tension traced back to the resignation of Winston Churchill after sustaining injuries during the bombing of dublin. His successor in the Tory party, perhaps without fully contemplating the consequences, had taken unilateral action. The decision involved seizing the remaining German nuclear weapons and transporting them back to Britain. Shockingly, this move was made without consultation with any of the allied nations, creating a significant rift.

As the political landscape evolved, the newly elected Labour Party, now in power, showed a surprising willingness to retain control over the acquired nuclear arsenal. Their motivation seemed to stem from concerns about the stability of the British Empire post-war, viewing the possession of these weapons as a means to uphold imperialistic control.

President Wallace found himself grappling with a situation he hadn't anticipated. The ideological struggle of capitalism versus communism had morphed into a complex dynamic of imperialism versus self-determination. The very foundations of the alliance forged during the war were being tested, and the emergence of a new kind of geopolitical conflict was leaving him bewildered and searching for answers. How had the path veered so drastically from their collective vision of a peaceful post-war world?

THE TWO PRESIDENTS

BENITO MUSSOLINI FOUND himself in a state of profound relief. The survival of his life was a testament to Italy's resilience, now positioned as the undisputed master of the Mediterranean, a revival of the glorious legacy of Rome. However, as he contemplated the new world order emerging after the war, questions lingered: What next?

Italy, despite its achievements, found itself overshadowed by the dominant superpowers—Britain and America. Mussolini, confined to a wheelchair due to the consequences of the Dublin bombing, realized the need for diplomatic finesse. Another war was out of the question; hence, he embarked on a diplomatic mission to secure Italy's interests.

Maneuvering his wheelchair, Il Duce contemplated how to navigate this post-war landscape. The scars of war, both physical and political, adorned him—a testament to his role as a seasoned diplomat. While grateful for his survival, Mussolini recognized that realigning Italy's position in the global power structure required strategic finesse.

Cursing Adolf Hitler for the bombing that left him permanently disabled, Mussolini saw an opportunity in his scars. Perhaps he could leverage his experiences as a diplomat and war survivor to forge a new diplomatic front. The key lay in playing Britain and America against each other, manipulating the delicate balance of power for Italy's benefit. The Il Duce understood that careful planning and skillful maneuvering were imperative to tread this narrow path successfully. The post-war world demanded a different kind of warfare, and Mussolini was determined to emerge victorious on the diplomatic front.

WINSTON CHURCHILL'S concern deepened as he observed the toxic rhetoric emanating from Westminster, creating a virulent atmosphere against the very allies with whom they had won a war. The abrupt shift in attitude puzzled him, and he couldn't help but wonder about the root cause of this drastic change.

As a private citizen now, Churchill tried to distance himself from the political fray, focusing on a more relaxed lifestyle much to his doctor's delight. The sip of brandy in his hand offered a familiar comfort, a vice he clung to despite the changing tides around him.

The seizure of the German nuclear arsenal by his successor did raise eyebrows, but Churchill attempted to dismiss such concerns. He chided himself for dwelling on matters that were no longer his responsibility. However, the deteriorating relations between Britain and America continued to linger in his thoughts.

Wistfully contemplating the past, Churchill found it challenging to ignore the alarming transformation in the alliance. If only Franklin Roosevelt were still alive, he believed, none of this discord would have unfolded.

Determined to stay on the sidelines, Churchill sensed that the evolving world order held unpredictable changes, catching everyone off guard. The veteran statesman couldn't escape the nagging thought that the world, in its newfound state, was hurtling towards an uncertain future.

Chapter 17

Words and Worlds apart

PUBLIC ANNOUNCEMENT
BY ORDER OF KING GEORGE VI
A GLORIOUS DECLARATION OF UNITY FOR THE
BRITISH EMPIRE

To our Grateful Subjects,

In the jubilant aftermath of a hard-fought victory, where the winds of unity have carried us through the tempests of war, I, King George VI, joyfully address you with a proclamation that heralds a new era of prosperity for our esteemed British Empire.

Behold the dawn of a unified destiny, as we proudly announce the establishment of a 'Unified' British Empire—a beacon of harmony, strength, and shared purpose. Today, we celebrate the collective spirit that binds our dominions, colonies, and realms into a harmonious symphony of collaboration and mutual respect.

With hearts brimming with patriotism, we affirm that this union is not one of coercion but a manifestation of our shared commitment to a brighter future. Embracing the unique identities of each territory, we unite under the common banner of progress, justice, and solidarity.

In this historic moment, we recognize the rich diversity of our empire as a source of strength, weaving a tapestry of cultures, traditions, and aspirations. As we stand united, we shall cherish our differences, drawing strength from the vast mosaic of our heritage, ensuring that every voice within our empire resonates with pride and purpose.

Let this proclamation resonate from the historic streets of London to the vast landscapes of Australasia, echoing through the valleys of Canada and reverberating within the vibrant cities of Africa and the Indian subcontinent. Together, we embark on a journey of shared prosperity, guided by the principles of democracy, justice, and equality for all.

May this announcement stand as a testament to the triumph of unity over division, a pledge to cultivate a future adorned with the fruits of collaboration and mutual understanding.

God Save the King, and May the Unified British Empire Flourish!

Given with unwavering optimism,

George R.

VICE PRESIDENT FREDRICK Mason was perplexed by the British Empire's unexpected shift towards unity. A "Unified" British Empire seemed counter to the historical trajectory of decolonization and the promotion of self-determination. What had triggered this divergence in the timeline? Deep down, he acknowledged that his interference, particularly with the deployment of nuclear weapons, had disrupted the natural course of events.

"Damn those cursed devices", he thought to himself, "he should have never accelerated their development."

Navigating his way through the hallowed halls of the White House, Mr. Mason entered the Oval Office to find President Wallace awaiting him.

"Like what I've done with the place?" President Wallace quipped, gesturing to the office's new furnishings.

"Oh, you've redecorated. I don't like it," Mr. Mason deadpanned.

"Really?" President Wallace questioned.

"Besides, you're going to have to gut the whole place in a few years anyway," Mr. Mason remarked casually.

"Why?" President Wallace inquired, raising an eyebrow.

"A piano is going to fall through one of the floors in 1948. Truman had to stay at the Blair House for half his presidency," Mr. Mason explained matter-of-factly.

Wallace slumped his shoulders, and Mr. Mason was almost certain he heard a muttered "damn it" under the president's breath.

"So, I take it you heard King George's royal proclamation?" Mr. Mason inquired.

"Of course," President Wallace replied. "It worries me greatly. I fear that Cold War you mentioned is going to happen one way or the other."

"But with Britain," Mr. Mason said in disbelief. "I never saw that coming. We always had a special relationship with them."

"Well, it's here," Wallace sighed, throwing up his hands. "What do we do?"

"Why are you asking me? You're the President."

"And you were once a president as well and are now vice-president. So, I get to ask you for help."

"Well, I'm not sure," Mr. Mason replied flatly.

"What do you mean you don't know?" President Wallace admonished.

"It means, I plainly don't know. This has never happened, and it isn't exactly an ideological struggle between capitalism and communism."

"Well, what the hell are we supposed to do then?" President Wallace demanded, slamming his hand down onto the desk.

Mr. Mason took a deep breath. "O.K, let me think. Quebec has always had an independent streak to it. With the right nudges, we could have them push for independence and can properly test the new Unified British Empire."

"Well then, let's make it so," President Wallace declared.

Mr. Mason leaned back in his chair, contemplating the complexities of this geopolitical chess match. "We need to be careful, though," he cautioned. "This isn't just about Quebec; it's about navigating a delicate diplomatic landscape. We want to assess their unity without causing irreparable damage."

President Wallace nodded in agreement. "Absolutely. We can't afford to start another conflict. Our goal is to understand the dynamics at play and perhaps find opportunities for cooperation rather than confrontation."

Mr. Mason continued, "We should discreetly support Quebec's push for autonomy. Keep it subtle, encourage dialogue, and observe how the Unified British Empire reacts. This way, we can gauge their internal strength and identify potential areas for collaboration."

President Wallace, though uneasy about the growing tensions, recognized the need for a nuanced approach. "Proceed cautiously, Fredrick. Let's not forget our shared history with Britain and the importance of maintaining a strong, stable alliance. But we also need to safeguard our national interests and principles."

As the plan took shape, both men understood the weight of their decisions. The future of international relations hung in the balance, and navigating this uncharted territory required finesse and strategic acumen.

Quebec Demands Independence Vote, Testing Unified British Empire's Resolve

By Anthony Bridger

April 10, 1945

In a bold move that has sent shockwaves through international diplomatic circles, Quebec has officially demanded an independence vote from the newly formed Unified British Empire. The Quebecois government, citing a desire for self-determination and autonomy, has called for a referendum to gauge the province's support for independence.

The announcement, made by Premier Maurice Duplessis, has added a new layer of complexity to the post-World War II geopolitical landscape. The Unified British Empire, a recently consolidated union of British nations, including Canada, is now faced with a significant challenge to its unity.

Observers note that Quebec's push for independence comes at a time when tensions between the United States and the Unified British Empire are already heightened. The move could be seen as a strategic play by the U.S. to test the cohesiveness of its former ally following the war.

Premier Duplessis, addressing the Quebecois public, emphasized the province's unique cultural and linguistic identity. He stated, "Quebec has its distinct heritage, and the time has come for us to decide our own destiny. We must shape our future according to the will of our people."

The Unified British Empire's response is eagerly awaited, as the international community speculates on how this demand for independence will be handled. Some anticipate a diplomatic resolution, emphasizing dialogue and understanding, while others fear the possibility of heightened tensions leading to a more significant conflict.

The unfolding events highlight the intricate challenges facing the world in the post-war era. As nations grapple with the aftermath of a devastating global conflict, the pursuit of national identity and self-determination takes center stage, bringing both hopes for peace and concerns for potential new conflicts.

WINSTON CHURCHILL WAS deeply troubled by the reports of conflict brewing in Canada, specifically the Quebec independence movement. The news struck a chord with him, as he grappled with conflicting emotions. On one hand, he had long championed the cause of self-determination, but on the other, the unfolding events seemed to challenge the principles of unity and cooperation he held dear.

His opposition to the Unified British Empire initiative was well-known, favoring instead a vision of a Commonwealth where nations freely associated with each other. Now, witnessing the consequences of this controversial move, Churchill couldn't help but feel a sense of foreboding. The conflict in Quebec, fueled by aspirations for independence, had deeper roots that extended beyond national boundaries.

Sitting in his study, Churchill mulled over the situation. He couldn't fathom the motivations behind Westminster's decision to consolidate power and territory under the banner of a unified empire. It appeared to him as an egregious departure from the principles that had guided the Allies in their fight against the totalitarian regimes of Hitler and Mussolini.

Fueled by a sense of urgency, Churchill attempted to rise from his chair, the effort intensified by the lingering effects of his injuries. Though physically challenged, his resolve remained unbroken. The gravity of the situation demanded action, and he felt compelled to use his influence to address what he perceived as a dangerous deviation from the values that had shaped the post-war world.

With a determination etched on his face, Churchill set his sights on making his voice heard, ready to contribute once again to the global discourse on the importance of liberty, self-determination, and cooperation among nations. He still had enough clout to get that at least. He would be heard and heard loudly at that.

Chapter 18

The conflict gets warm

THINGS WERE TAKING a turn for the worse, and the situation could only be described as chaotic. The carefully executed plan to stir up trouble in Quebec had backfired spectacularly, with the province now teetering on the brink of open rebellion. The flames of defiance were spreading, with a surge in southern sympathy and nationalism creating a headache for the Federal government. It was a taste of their own medicine, and it tasted bitter.

Despite a strong inclination to blame the Unified British Empire for funding these movements, Fredrick Mason knew better. The southern uprising appeared to be organic, a grassroots expression of discontent that had outpaced their expectations. His attempts to introduce more civil rights during the Roosevelt and Wallace administrations had hit a brick wall in the South, leaving him frustrated and in desperate need of a solution.

Comparatively, the situation in the United States seemed less dire than the struggles faced by the British. Yet, the emerging Cold War was an unwelcome development, a feeble imitation of the historical conflict he had learned about in history class. Mr. Mason gave it a one out of five stars, finding it to be a weak facsimile of the original.

Amidst the turmoil, there was a glimmer of hope and a personal commitment that Mr. Mason clung to. The moonshot, a promise he had made to Wernher von Braun, was still on the horizon. Despite numerous war-related delays, he was determined to fulfill this ambitious plan for a manned lunar program. In just two weeks, a Saturn V-like vehicle would embark on a historic journey to the moon, landing three men on its surface. It may look different from the Apollo Program of history, but that was the consequence of starting it twenty-five years ahead of schedule.

Waiting in the Oval Office for President Wallace's return, Mr. Mason's anticipation was abruptly shattered by the entrance of an exasperated aide.

"What is the meaning of this?" demanded Mr. Mason.

"It's... It's Winston Churchill. He's been assassinated."

Tragedy Strikes: Churchill Falls Victim to Unlikely Assassins

By Anthony Bridger
August 15, 1945

In a shocking turn of events, the world was left stunned as news broke of the assassination of Winston Churchill on August 15, 1945. What makes this tragedy even more perplexing is that the perpetrators are believed to be Quebec nationalists, a group ostensibly aligned with Churchill's ideals of self-determination and liberty.

The iconic British statesman, who played a pivotal role in leading the Allies to victory in World War II, had been a vocal advocate for the rights of nations to determine their own destinies. However, in the post-war period, Churchill found himself at odds with the newly established Unified British Empire, a controversial initiative that aimed to consolidate power within the British Isles.

Churchill's opposition to this move had not gone unnoticed, and tensions had been escalating. The catalyst for this shocking act of violence appears to be rooted in the complex dynamics surrounding Quebec's struggle for independence. While the motives of the Quebec nationalists remain the subject of intense speculation, it is clear that their actions have sent shockwaves through the international community.

As news of Churchill's assassination reverberated globally, leaders from across the Allied nations expressed their condolences and condemned the act. President Henry Wallace of the United States, who had previously served as Vice President under Churchill's wartime ally Franklin D. Roosevelt, expressed his deep sorrow at the loss of a key figure in the fight against tyranny.

The motivations behind this unprecedented act are raising questions about the complexities of post-war geopolitics. It remains to be seen how this tragic event will impact relations between the Unified British Empire and other nations, especially as the world grapples with rebuilding and establishing a new order after the ravages of war.

The assassination of Winston Churchill serves as a stark reminder that even those who fought side by side in the struggle against fascism are not immune to the challenges of shaping a post-war world. As the investigation into this shocking incident unfolds, the world watches with bated breath, grappling with the implications of a turbulent and uncertain future.

"WE NEED TO CUT ALL aid to these Quebec nationalists immediately," demanded President Wallace.

"Already done, sir," Mr. Mason replied.

"Good. We can't be associated with this in any way. The assassination of Churchill has altered the landscape significantly."

"Yes, I'm well aware," replied Mr. Mason, somewhat annoyed.

"Do we have any idea which group in Quebec is behind the attack?"

"No, we don't. What we do know is that sympathy for Quebec independence has all but collapsed. People are turning their backs on them for conducting what seems to have been a misguided attack."

"And what about British troops?"

"They are blockading Quebec and have laid a dual siege to both Montreal and Quebec City."

"I still don't know what they were thinking," President Wallace said, shaking his head.

"They were probably thinking the U.S is giving us aid; they have our backs. We can attempt to make a big move and gain headlines, and they will support us. I don't think they thought they would succeed and were not prepared for the consequences."

"Hmmm, that seems a bit specific," President Wallace said skeptically.

"It's happened several times in history, both in the past and in the future."

President Wallace slumped into his chair, exhaling loudly. "That may be so. What about the situation in the south?"

"Well, paradoxically, the siege of Quebec seems to have emboldened some of the louder elements there."

"Of course it did," President Wallace said, annoyed. "What can we do?"

"Honestly," Mr. Mason said slowly, "I don't think there is anything we can do."

"What?" President Wallace said, sitting up. "What do you mean nothing?"

"Well," Mr. Mason began to explain, "with the British distracted by Quebec, as well as some minor uprisings in Africa, tensions between us and them are at an all-time low since the end of the war. I'm afraid to say it, but the South is a home-grown problem."

"Well, that's just perfect," President Wallace said, crossing his arms. "We win the biggest war in history and are at the top of the world, and what do we do? We snatch defeat from the jaws of victory."

"I just don't know what we can do here," Mr. Mason admitted honestly.

President Wallace looked at Mr. Mason solemnly, as if realizing something. "We prepare for the worst. Why don't you go home and get some rest? I think it's going to be the last you're going to get for a while."

"Sir," Mr. Mason asked, confused.

"It's just a feeling I have. I don't know why, though."

Mr. Mason stared at the president for a few moments before deciding to go along with whatever the president said. "Have a good rest of your day, sir."

"Goodbye, Frederick," the president replied. This was the first time the man had ever referred to him as just Frederick, and not as Mr. Mason or his full name.

Unrest in the Southern States: Nationalism on the Rise
By Anthony Bridger
September 10, 1945

As the echoes of World War II's victorious crescendo began to fade, a different battlefront is emerging in the United States – one rooted in the complex history and social fabric of the southern states. The aftermath of the war, coupled with attempts at wartime civil rights reforms, has ignited a fervent nationalism, taking hold in the heart of Dixie.

The southern states, once at the epicenter of the conflict over slavery, were now grappling with a new challenge: adapting to a post-war era marked by changing social dynamics and the push for greater civil rights. President Wallace's administration, cognizant of the need for reform, attempted to address racial inequality through a series of measures.

However, these reforms, instead of fostering unity, have become a catalyst for rising nationalism and resistance in the South. The region, deeply entrenched in its traditions and historical identity, has responded with defiance to what some perceive as an intrusion into their way of life.

The post-war period has witnessed a paradoxical surge in nationalism, a phenomenon fueled not only by a perceived external threat but also by a desire to maintain the status quo. The very reforms designed to bring about positive change have unintentionally fanned the flames of discontent.

Southern sympathizers, viewing the reforms as an infringement on their autonomy, have organized in opposition. The attempts to integrate schools and workplaces, dismantle segregation, and guarantee voting rights to all citizens are met with vehement resistance.

Furthermore, the situation in the South has been exacerbated by external factors. The recent events in Quebec and the assassination of Winston Churchill have led to increased tension between the United States and its former ally, the United British Empire. This global turmoil is reflected in the internal strife of the southern states.

As the nation struggles to find its footing in this post-war era, the question of whether the South will embrace change or resist it remains unanswered. The coming months will undoubtedly be crucial in shaping the destiny of a nation that fought against tyranny abroad but now faces the challenges of unity and equality on its own soil.

THE SHRILL RING OF the telephone jolted Fredrick Mason from a vivid dream, thrusting him from the triumphant echoes of a 2045 victory speech back into the stark reality of 1945. Disoriented and still half-submerged in the remnants of the dream, he fumbled to answer.

"Hello?" he mumbled, his voice thick with sleep.

"Sir, you need to make your way to the White House this instant," the urgent voice on the other end demanded.

"Why? What's going on?" Mr. Mason queried, his drowsiness replaced by an immediate alertness. The tone of the caller hinted at impending gravity, reminiscent of the news that had shattered his sleep just days before – the assassination of Winston Churchill.

"It's President Wallace. He's dead."

Chapter 19

Into the Fire

THE WORDS HUNG HEAVILY in the air, cutting through the stillness of the room. The abrupt news sent a chill down Mr. Mason's spine, banishing any remnants of drowsiness. In that instant, the dreams of a better tomorrow, the echoes of victory, all faded away, replaced by the stark reality that the nation was once again thrust into uncertainty. With a sense of foreboding, Mr. Mason quickly gathered his senses, realizing that the tumultuous events of recent days were far from over. The weight of responsibility pressed upon him as he prepared to face a new chapter in this turbulent journey through time.

Hanging up the phone with an abrupt force that matched the gravity of the news, Fredrick Mason roused his wife Bailey from her peaceful slumber to share the shocking update. In the dimly lit room, sleep was quickly dispelled by the stark reality that awaited them.

"Bailey," he whispered urgently, "you won't believe what's happened. President Wallace is dead."

Her eyes widened in disbelief as the weight of the news settled in. Quickly discarding their nightclothes, they both hurriedly dressed, the urgency of the situation palpable in the air.

As buttons were fastened and ties secured, Bailey looked at her husband with a gaze that reflected both concern and realization. "Fredrick," she said pointedly, "you are the president again."

The words hung in the air, resonating with a weighty truth that neither of them could escape. Once again, the mantle of leadership had been thrust upon Fredrick Mason. He hadn't actively considered the implications until Bailey voiced it, but now the gravity of the situation became undeniable.

With a final glance at themselves in the mirror, they stepped outside their home, where an unexpected vehicle awaited their departure. Though the surprise was genuine, the presence of the waiting transport seemed strangely fitting. After confirming their identities, they entered the vehicle, the engine's hum marking the beginning of a journey back to the heart of political power – the White House.

As the vehicle navigated through the early morning streets, Fredrick held Bailey's hand tightly, a silent reassurance amid the whirlwind of thoughts racing through his mind. How had he found himself in this position once again? What would the world say when the news broke? Uncertainties loomed on the horizon, but one thing was clear – a new chapter awaited them within the hallowed walls of the White House, and Fredrick Mason was about to lead the nation once more into an uncertain future.

Tragic Loss: President Wallace's Death Shrouded in Mystery: Nation Mourns as Investigations Begin into the Sudden Demise

By Anthony Bridger

THE TWO PRESIDENTS

November 1, 1945

In a shocking turn of events, President Henry Wallace has passed away, leaving the nation in mourning and uncertainty. The circumstances surrounding his death are currently under investigation, with initial suspicions pointing towards the rising wave of southern nationalism.

President Wallace, who had taken office at the end of World War II, was found lifeless earlier today, leaving a void at the heart of the nation. The cause of death remains elusive, as authorities delve into the details surrounding this unexpected tragedy.

As news of his demise spread, a somber atmosphere descended over the country, and citizens from coast to coast grappled with the loss of a leader who had guided them through the tumultuous times of war.

The investigation is focusing on the possibility of southern nationalist sentiments playing a role in the untimely death of the President. Tensions in the southern states have been escalating in recent months, fueled by both internal and external factors. The President's demise, occurring amid these heightened tensions, has raised questions about the potential involvement of extremist elements.

Authorities are working diligently to unravel the circumstances leading to President Wallace's death, and the nation eagerly awaits answers during this period of mourning. The sudden shift in the political landscape has left the country on edge, and citizens are anxiously awaiting official statements from investigative agencies.

As the nation grapples with grief and uncertainty, the legacy of President Wallace looms large. A dedicated public servant, Wallace's vision for a better world will be remembered, and his untimely death casts a shadow over the future trajectory of the United States. Vice President Mason has assumed the office of President.

THE INAUGURATION CEREMONY had been swift, reminiscent of the speed with which President Wallace ascended to power after Roosevelt's demise. President Mason found himself rapidly ushered to the newly constructed situation room, where a grim revelation awaited him.

"We suspect President Wallace was poisoned," a staff member divulged.

"What?" President Mason exclaimed.

"Out of public view, we believe an infiltrator from a group known as the Sons of the New Confederacy managed to slip poison into his meal. We've been monitoring this group for some time," the staffer explained.

"Henry never breathed a word about this," Mr. Mason scolded.

"No, he wanted to avoid causing a panic, for both the public and you. He believed you already had a lot on your plate," came the response.

"Oh, Henry," President Mason sighed, shaking his head. He took a deep breath. "Okay, listen up. This is not how we operate moving forward. I want a press release drafted for tomorrow, outlining our concerns and identifying who we believe is responsible. Is that understood?" A murmur spread through the room. "I asked if that is understood," President Mason reiterated, demanding a clearer response. The room echoed with a more resounding acknowledgment.

The gravity of the situation weighed heavily on President Mason's shoulders. A plot to poison the President, coupled with the Sons of the New Confederacy's involvement, set a dire tone for the beginning of his unexpected term. Determined to confront the challenge head-on, he made it clear that transparency would be the cornerstone of his administration's response. They had to if the United States were to survive as a nation.

Assassination of President Wallace Shocks the Nation

By Anthony Bridger
November 2, 1945

In a shocking turn of events, President Henry Wallace's sudden death has been attributed to a poisoning attempt. The news, kept confidential until now, has rattled the nation and cast a shadow of uncertainty over the political landscape.

President Wallace, who had recently been sworn in for a second term earlier in, he year, succumbed to the effects of the poison, prompting an immediate investigation by federal authorities. The suspected culprit is believed to be a member of a clandestine group known as the Sons of the New Confederacy. This revelation has sent shockwaves through the government, with President Wallace's successor, Fredrick Mason, vowing to address the situation with transparency and urgency.

The Sons of the New Confederacy, a fringe organization advocating for extreme nationalist ideologies, has long been under surveillance by intelligence agencies. The motive behind the poisoning appears to be rooted in rising southern nationalism, as tensions escalate in the aftermath of World War II.

President Mason, addressing the nation earlier today, expressed his commitment to a thorough investigation and promised to keep the public informed. "This heinous act will not go unanswered," President Mason declared. "We will bring those responsible to justice, and we will do so with the utmost transparency."

The President's death has triggered a wave of condolences from world leaders, reflecting the global impact of this unexpected tragedy. The circumstances surrounding Wallace's poisoning and the subsequent rise in southern nationalism raise concerns about the stability of the United States in the post-war era.

As the nation mourns the loss of President Wallace, questions linger about the Sons of the New Confederacy and their potential influence on domestic affairs. The weeks ahead promise to be challenging as the United States grapples with both mourning its fallen leader and navigating the uncertain political waters that lie ahead.

PRESIDENT MASON'S RETURN to office proved to be a formidable challenge as he grappled with a trifecta of crises: the investigation into President Wallace's assassination, the escalating southern crisis, and the ongoing siege of Quebec. Each day seemed to bring a new set of challenges, and the weight of the unforeseen events bore heavily on Mason's shoulders.

As he prepared for bed, Bailey, his steadfast partner, joined him. Her discerning eye, honed in the world of 2045, wasn't entirely impressed with the new security detail assigned to protect the President in this bygone era.

"I think I ran a much tighter ship back in 2045," Bailey remarked.

"Well, how are they doing for the 1940s?" Fredrick inquired.

"O.K., I guess," she conceded.

"Then that's what matters," he replied, trying to find solace in the fact that, despite the unfamiliar territory, his security detail was holding its ground.

Bailey, however, wasn't easily swayed. "Not really," she countered. "So how are you adjusting now that you're back in the job?"

Turning back to face his wife, Fredrick, who had been lying on his side, sighed. "Well, I've stolen Eisenhower's presidential number, come into power in the wake of several high-profile assassinations, and there's a war to our north, with another one brewing to our south."

"So, not good, then, I take it," Bailey said humorously.

"Exactly," the President rolled back over. "I think I just need some sleep," he declared.

"Then I won't stop you," Bailey replied, leaning down and kissing Fredrick on the cheek. She then reached over and turned off the lights before settling into bed herself.

Civil War! Secession Announcements Shake the Nation
By Anthony Bridger
November 11, 1945

In an astonishing turn of events, the Southern states of Alabama, South Carolina, Georgia, and Mississippi have collectively declared their secession from the United States, plunging the nation into a fresh crisis following the recent assassination of President Henry Wallace.

The roots of this unprecedented move can be traced back to the complex aftermath of World War II. While the war united the nation in the face of a common enemy, the ensuing struggle for equality and civil rights has revealed deep-seated divisions. The Southern states, resistant to the wartime civil rights improvements championed by Presidents Roosevelt and Wallace, have opted for secession as a means of expressing their discontent.

THE TWO PRESIDENTS

President Fredrick Mason, who recently assumed office in the aftermath of President Wallace's tragic death, is now faced with the daunting task of preserving the unity of the nation.

The decision by these Southern states to secede highlights the ongoing tensions between the regions, aggravated by the societal changes initiated during the war. The attempt to address systemic racial inequalities through civil rights reforms has generated opposition, resulting in a drastic move toward secession as a demonstration of defiance.

As news of the secession spreads, concerns arise about the potential for renewed civil conflict and the impact on the fragile global order established after the war. The international community watches with trepidation as a member state threatens to disrupt the delicate balance achieved through the formation of the United Nations.

President Mason, navigating the turbulent waters of this unforeseen crisis, must now find a way to reconcile the divisions within the nation. The secession of these Southern states serves as a stark reminder that the aftermath of war involves not only rebuilding physical structures but also addressing the underlying social and political issues that persist long after the cessation of hostilities. The fate of the United States hangs in the balance as the nation grapples with this unforeseen and formidable challenge.

Chapter 20

The Tunnel

PRESIDENT FREDRICK Mason found himself grappling with the weight of an unprecedented crisis, one that bore the heavy burden of consequences resulting from his actions. The magnitude of the situation was almost too overwhelming for the man from the future to bear. Millions had lost their lives, and a nation once on the path to healing now stood in the path of a devastating civil war.

The Southern states of North Carolina, Florida, Louisiana, and Arkansas had cast their lot with those who sought secession, sending shockwaves through the nation. The announcement of disunion reverberated like a thunderclap, shaking the very foundations of the Union. However, amidst the turmoil, there was an unexpected glimmer of hope. Virginia, Tennessee, and Texas had declared their allegiance to the Union, providing some relief in the face of overwhelming adversity.

Yet, even with this unexpected loyalty, President Mason couldn't escape the reality that his decisions had played a significant role in triggering this crisis. The repercussions of his actions were unfolding before him, a nightmare come to life that surpassed any he could have imagined. The gravity of the situation weighed heavily on his shoulders.

As he grappled with the enormity of the crisis, President Mason couldn't help but wonder how he would navigate these treacherous waters. The specter of a civil war loomed ominously, threatening to tear the nation apart. This, undoubtedly, was a far cry from the future he had hoped to create. The delicate balance between states loyal to the Union and those seeking secession presented an intricate challenge that required delicate handling.

In the midst of this turmoil, President Mason's mind drifted to the possibility of World War III, an even more catastrophic scenario that lurked on the horizon. The challenges ahead were daunting, and the man from the future found himself at a crossroads, grappling with the consequences of his actions and the uncertain path that lay ahead for the United States.

President Fredrick Mason harbored a glimmer of optimism as he awaited General MacArthur's return from Japan. The prospect of cooperation with the esteemed general offered a ray of hope in navigating the tumultuous times that had befallen the nation. Mason recognized that if such collaboration were to materialize, the presidency would inevitably pass into MacArthur's capable hands in the coming years. It was a transition he looked forward to, a belief rooted in the trust he placed in the general's leadership.

Despite being in office for a mere month, the weight of the challenges had already taken its toll on Fredrick Mason. The presidency, fraught with complexities and crises, had proven more demanding than he could have envisioned. The decision to abstain from seeking re-election in 1948 had been a deliberate one, borne out of a pragmatic assessment of the arduous road ahead. Mason found solace in the notion that if he and the nation emerged from the trials relatively unscathed, it would be a victory in itself.

The exhaustion etched on Mason's face reflected the gravity of the circumstances. His commitment to steering the country through the storm was unwavering, but the toll on his energy and resolve was palpable. As he awaited the return of General MacArthur, President Mason held onto the hope that the collaboration he envisioned would bring stability to the nation, paving the way for a smoother transition in the years to come. The prospect of handing over the reins to a trusted leader offered a glimmer of relief amid the relentless challenges that defined his early days in the presidency. How would the American people see this?

General MacArthur Assumes Supreme Union Commander Role

By Anthony Bridger
December 8, 1945

In a monumental move aimed at navigating the storm of challenges facing the United States, President Fredrick Mason has appointed General Douglas MacArthur as the Supreme Union Commander. This significant position not only places General MacArthur at the forefront of military strategy but also grants him unprecedented access to the nation's nuclear arsenal.

President Mason's decision comes at a critical juncture as secessionist movements and internal strife threaten the unity of the nation. The President, acknowledging the need for a decisive and seasoned leader, turned to General MacArthur, whose illustrious military career and strategic acumen have earned him widespread respect.

The appointment signifies a departure from traditional norms, as General MacArthur assumes a role that blends military and strategic command with authority over the nation's nuclear capabilities. This move reflects the urgency of the situation and the necessity for a unified response to the multifaceted challenges confronting the country.

General MacArthur, known for his role in the Pacific during World War II, brings a wealth of experience and a reputation for disciplined leadership to this pivotal position. President Mason expressed his confidence in General MacArthur's ability to steer the nation through these turbulent times and safeguard its interests.

With this appointment, General MacArthur is entrusted with coordinating military efforts, managing internal strife, and, critically, having access to nuclear weapons to deter potential adversaries. The decision underscores the gravity of the challenges faced by the United States and the imperative for a comprehensive strategy to maintain stability and preserve the Union.

As the nation watches with bated breath, General MacArthur assumes his new role with a weighty responsibility. The Supreme Union Commander's ability to navigate these complex times will undoubtedly shape the course of history, determining the fate of a nation grappling with internal dissent and external uncertainties.

IN A PIVOTAL MOMENT echoing the decisions of President Truman during World War II, President Mason found himself grappling with the weighty choice of authorizing the use of nuclear weapons on American soil against secessionist states. Wrestling with the moral dilemma of unleashing such destructive force on U.S. citizens, even those in rebellion, President Mason deliberated for days before reluctantly giving General MacArthur the green light, albeit with stringent conditions.

The prospect of employing nuclear weapons carried with it a potent shock factor that could potentially expedite the resolution of the conflict. However, President Mason couldn't shake the profound concern for the potential human cost and the lasting repercussions of such a decision. As he penned the orders that could reshape the course of the civil war, he couldn't help but wonder if he had just signed off on a colossal mistake.

Burdened by the weight of the decision, President Mason buried his head in his hands, contemplating the complex calculus of war, morality, and the preservation of the Union. He knew that, regardless of the outcome, history would judge him harshly. Yet, after enduring the relentless challenges of altering the past and steering a troubled nation, he found himself at a point where he had become somewhat indifferent to the opinions of posterity. In a world marked by the scars of war and the echoes of historical revisions, President Mason had reached a place where he simply didn't give a damn anymore.

Nuclear Detonations Bring Secessionist States to Heel

THE TWO PRESIDENTS

By Anthony Bridger
January 1, 1946

In a shocking turn of events that unfolded at the stroke of midnight to usher in the new year, four major cities—Little Rock, Atlanta, Charlotte, and Tallahassee—witnessed the detonation of nuclear weapons, compelling secessionist states to capitulate to the Union's demands.

The unprecedented use of nuclear weapons marks a dark chapter in American history and signals the lengths to which the government is willing to go to maintain the Union's integrity. The decision to deploy such destructive force underscores the severity of the internal strife that has plagued the nation in recent months.

Reports indicate that the nuclear detonations were strategically targeted to instigate surrender rather than inflict widespread destruction. President Fredrick Mason, who announced the military action, defended the decision, emphasizing the imperative to quell secessionist movements that threatened the very fabric of the nation.

While the casualties and impact on the affected cities are still being assessed, the swift surrender of the secessionist states—North Carolina, Florida, Louisiana, Arkansas, and others—is undeniable. The shockwaves from the nuclear detonations reverberated through the secessionist leadership, prompting them to reconsider their stance and submit to the might of the Union.

President Mason, in a somber address to the nation, expressed regret at resorting to such extreme measures but maintained that it was a necessary step to preserve the Union. He emphasized the importance of reestablishing unity and rebuilding the fractured nation in the aftermath of this unprecedented event.

The international community watches with a mix of astonishment and concern as the United States grapples with internal strife on an unparalleled scale. The aftermath of these nuclear detonations will undoubtedly shape the trajectory of the nation, influencing its domestic policies and international standing.

As the country confronts the aftermath of this harrowing event, questions arise about the potential long-term consequences and the impact on the American psyche. The use of nuclear weapons within its borders leaves an indelible mark on the nation, challenging its values and resilience as it strives to overcome this tumultuous period in its history.

THE BURDEN OF THE DECISIONS forced upon him during the second American Civil War weighed heavily on President Mason's shoulders, pushing him to the brink of what he could endure. Despite the relatively short duration of the conflict, the toll it took in terms of civilian casualties, a consequence he had authorized, far surpassed that of the first Civil War. The weight of such decisions, particularly those involving the loss of innocent lives, gnawed at President Mason's conscience, plunging his mental health to an all-time low.

In the stillness of the night, President Mason found himself unable to escape the haunting consequences of his choices. Staring at the ceiling in a state of sleeplessness, he sought solace in silent prayers, pleading with a higher power for forgiveness. The weight of his actions felt like a curse he longed to be lifted, as he grappled with growing paranoia and an intense desire for an honorable way out of the internal turmoil.

However, amidst the personal struggle, President Mason was acutely aware that he still had a duty to fulfill. Determined to uphold the oath he took to serve the American people, he pressed on despite the mental toll. When interacting with the public, he donned a metaphorical mask, concealing his inner struggles of depression and anxiety. In the public eye, he aimed to be the everyman's president, putting forth a facade of strength and commitment even as the emotional weight of his decisions bore down on him.

As President Mason exerted his utmost efforts to fulfill his duty to the American people, an incessant worry plagued his thoughts—what would come next under his watch? The weight of responsibility for the chaos around him, a new Cold War, and the harrowing nuclear civil war, bore down on him incessantly. Despite yearning for a respite, the notion of returning home eluded him, trapped in the throes of a relentless and unforgiving reality.

In the quiet moments when his mind had a moment to itself, an expletive echoed within President Mason's thoughts, reflecting the frustration and helplessness that he grappled with.

"Fuck," he mused, recognizing the inadequacy of this sentiment in the face of the overwhelming challenges he confronted. Yet, it was the only release, the only expression that captured the tumultuous storm within. The president was left grappling with the consequences of decisions that had spiraled out of control, yearning for a reprieve that remained stubbornly out of reach.

"Just Fuck."

THE END

About the Author

Joseph Boro is a lover on History, having gotten his bachelors degree in the subject at the University of Central Florida. He often thinks about the what if's, and wishes to tell both this and real history to those who will listen.

About the Publisher

Boro Publishing, LLC is a small independent publisher, seeking to tell stories, both real and fictional. We want to tell everyone's story, and do it in the best way possible.